Kenny,

May your treasure
chest overflow with all
the riches you desire.

Joey

PIRATES OF FINANCIAL FREEDOM

PIRATES OF FINANCIAL FREEDOM

A Novel

JOEY FEHRMAN

LUDUS MEDIA

Cover designed by R'tor John Maghuyop
Pirates of Financial Freedom Compass Logo designed by Darren Rutledge
Typesetting by Christopher Derrick
Ludus Media logo design by Moch. Yusuf Kurniawan
Headshot photographed by Victoria Janashvili
Editors of various drafts: Winslow Eliot, Tracy Seybold, and Jennifer Eolin

ISBN: 978-0-9915474-0-1

Library of Congress Control Number: 2014902797

Printed in the United States of America

10 9 8 7 6 5 4 3 2 1
First edition

Dedicated to my parents and sister.
Thank you for always being there for me.

Author's Note

Are you ready to take control of your financial life and have fun in the process? Then get ready to experience a financial literacy adventure unlike any other!

Whether you know nothing about money or you've read a few other personal finance books, this novel can take you to the next level. I have studied financial and investing concepts for years, and I've filled this book with some of the most effective fundamental tips I have discovered. More importantly, it is designed to get you to take action. Simply knowing a concept isn't enough. To see real change in your life, you need to apply those concepts. And that is exactly what I want: for you to take control of your financial destiny.

You are not only helping yourself by buying this book, you are helping others as well. I talk about the importance of giving to charity in this novel, and I am putting this advice into action. Ten percent of all gross sales from this book will go to charity. The money will go to a variety of charities of my choice, and they are all great causes.

I have worked very hard on this novel, and I think you're going to love it. But I am committed to making it even better. I want this to be a timeless classic that can change the lives of countless people, and you can help make that happen. If you see anything that can be improved, whether it is the plot, financial concepts, something to add/delete, typos, etc, please send them to improvements@POFFbook.com.

Get excited, because this novel is both educational and entertaining, a concept known as edutainment. Edutainment is powerful because it makes the material easier to understand, less intimidating, more memorable, and it's simply just more fun. I feel it can change education in this country for the better, and I hope this book inspires others to write additional edutainment material.

This book will give you a solid foundation to essential personal finance skills. My dream is for this novel to change the direction of your financial life in ways you can't even believe. As the compass logo on the cover implies, if you follow the directions in this book they will lead you to lots of money. And I would love to hear your success stories! Please send them to me at success@POFFbook.com.

Now, turn the page for an action-packed adventure story that can bring you the financial freedom of your dreams.

Pirates of Financial Freedom

CHAPTER ONE

Fire the cannons!" The pirate ship rocked with the explosive blasts of eight cannons firing simultaneously. The projectiles rocketed toward the enemy ship, but only one was a direct hit. Minutes earlier, their adversaries had ambushed them, coming out of nowhere in the night fog. The captain was satisfied with one hit, considering they had such little time to prepare.

Flashes of light and smoke emanated from across the rift between the two vessels. "Brace for impact!" the captain shouted.

The crew dove for cover as the cannon fire crashed into their wooden hull and cut through one of the main masts. They were taking damage quickly, but the captain maneuvered through the night's ocean waters with expert skill. He aligned his ship to score severe damage to their enemy. "Fire!" he shouted.

"All the cannons don't be loaded yet, Captain!" shouted back one of the crew.

He slammed his fist in frustration. "Argh. Fire what yar got!"

Two cannons fired on the enemy ship, one scoring a solid hit. The captain didn't have much time before their attacker returned fire, and since his crew was short-handed, he knew this was a battle he couldn't win.

"Abort the mission! Head north by northwest!" They steered the ship away and got a good distance before they heard the blasts again. Cannon fire rained down around their ship, causing more damage. They set the sails to catch as much wind as possible, then sailed full-speed ahead. The enemy pursued but was no match for the fastest ship on the sea.

Feeling defeated, Captain Rich R. Dailey sat down on the deck and pondered his next move.

CHAPTER TWO

Owen entered the tavern and looked around. The place was a hole-in-the-wall with a consistently bad stench, but it was one of the few places left in town that still served pirates. The bullet holes in the wall, hook scratches on the chairs, and indentations covering the wooden floor all seemed normal to him.

Rusty sat at the bar, wearing his usual goofy grin as he gulped down his rum.

Owen walked over and took a seat next to Rusty. "What do the captain be wantin' at this hour of the morning?" he complained, having just rolled out of bed ten minutes earlier. He hated getting up before noon on a Saturday.

"I hope it be to buy us some rounds of rum," said Rusty hopefully. Twenty-one-year-old Rusty was the youngest member of Captain Dailey's crew. Though he was full of optimism, his childish striped red pants reflected his lack of experience. He was clean-shaven with short brown hair and brown eyes. His black vest was a couple sizes too big and looked baggy on his thin frame.

Owen grunted as he adjusted his stylish tricorn hat. Of the current crew, he had served the longest with the captain. He was a shorter man in his late twenties and wore an eye patch. Even though it was summer, his outfit was all black, which matched the color of his thick beard. He ordered a glass of premium Jamaican rum on the rocks.

The bartender brought Rusty a second glass of coconut-flavored rum mixed with pineapple juice. No sooner had they taken their first sips than the tavern doors burst open, revealing Ivan and Macon.

Owen scowled at them.

"Well, look who it be," said Ivan as he walked in. Ivan "Patch" Hurtz was a member of the rival Captain Goodman's crew. He wore dark clothing with an eye-patch and a purple bandana. His slightly-overweight build added to his intimidating look. It was said that he was born a landlubber and only recently became a pirate, which was in line with his reputation for being a bully.

"What be happenin' the other day?" asked Macon as he walked over to them. Macon Paine was another new member of Captain Goodman's crew. He followed Ivan around constantly and was rarely seen without him. He was taller and skinnier than Ivan, though wore a similar outfit with a matching purple bandana.

Macon punched Owen hard in the arm, causing Owen to spring to his feet.

"You can't be winnin' a sea fight but you think you can beat us in a land fight, aye?" laughed Ivan.

Macon laughed too, even harder than Ivan.

Captain Rich R. Dailey walked into the tavern.

"We be finishing this later," said Ivan, and they turned away to take a seat in the far corner. Even though they didn't like Captain Dailey, they respected him enough to not insult or injure his crew right in front of him.

The captain walked toward the bar. He was a tall man who wore traditional pirate garb: a black coat, red undershirt, long black boots, and a large hat. He wore an ornate golden key around his neck. He sat down next to Owen and Rusty. "Avast, me hearties." The captain gave a half-smile, which showed through his graying black beard. The wrinkles around his eyes looked more pronounced than usual, and he seemed stressed.

"What be wrong?" asked Rusty.

The captain glanced over at Ivan and Macon. "We just barely be escaping the battle with Captain Goodman the other day. That be the second time, and we can't let it happen again."

"It be because we're short on crew," said Owen, shaking his

head. "Captain Goodman be wreaking more and more havoc and doesn't seem to be stopping."

"Aye, only I can stop it. But to do it we be needing a bigger crew," Captain Dailey replied.

"That's what we've been trying to do," objected Owen. "But pirates be harder to come by nowadays. So many be leaving our unspoiled lifestyle behind, choosing to become landlubbers with their office jobs, cell phones, and modern ways." He spit on the ground in disgust. "Betrayers is what they be."

"I be trying to recruit more crew, Captain," said Rusty. "But those landlubbers don't want to join, even when I tell them all the benefits."

The idea of promoting benefits to help with recruitment caused the captain to sit up straighter. "Which benefits do you tell them about?"

"The best ones. I told 'em you don't need to shower. If ya lose yer hand ya get to wear a hook. And ye get to pee off the side of the boat whenever ya want. But they don't be interested." Rusty couldn't understand why everyone wasn't excited by those perks.

The captain shook his head. "They don't be caring about them benefits."

"What are we gonna do then?" asked Owen. "We be workin' like dogs since you fired the last crewmember." They all paused upon hearing Owen's comment since the firing topic was a sensitive issue. "You be regrettin' that decision now?"

The captain sighed. "There be no way I could have known what would happen afterwards. But at the time, it be the right decision to fire her."

"No sense in worrying about that now," said Rusty. "We be needing to come up with a plan for here forward."

"That's why I called you here," said the captain. "I figured out what landlubbers want. And it be the same thing us pirates want."

Rusty and Owen leaned forward to hear the answer.

The captain whispered, "Treasure."

At the sound of this magical word, their eyes widened and a grin spread across both their faces.

"They be wanting the pieces of eight, just like us," the captain continued. "If I can show them how much treasure me crew be having, they'll line up to join us."

Rusty became excited at the thought. "Great idea," he exclaimed. His excitement quickly turned to doubt. "But we be your crew, Captain. And we be broke." His body slumped in disappointment.

"Aye, and that be the problem. You all have plundered much treasure over the years, but have nothing to show for it. I bet you don't even know what you spent it on." The captain sighed heavily. "So I reached out to the only person I be knowing who could help."

"Who?" sneered Owen.

The captain turned his head. "Me son, Giuseppe."

The corner of Owen's lip tightened upon hearing this. "Giuseppe? What he be coming here for? Didn't you say he stormed out the last time you be seeing him, cursing our pirate ways and vowing never to come back?"

"He didn't be saying that exactly. He be saying he wouldn't come back unless—"

"Aye, I remember what he be demanding. You don't be accepting his terms, did ya now?" Owen said in an accusatory tone.

"Aye," replied the captain with a heavy heart.

"What you be thinking!" exclaimed Owen. "You swore to me you'd never stop. Why you be succumbing to his demands after all this time?"

The captain slammed his fist on the table. "Don't you be lecturing me. It be me only choice."

Rusty looked at them in confusion. "What's going on with Giuseppe? Captain, you always be saying good things about him and how you be wanting to see him."

"Aye," said the captain. "I be caring for me son, and I always be inviting him to see me. But he'd always refuse. He could never get over old wounds."

"So how'd ye get him here?" Rusty scratched his head as he thought of ways the captain might motivate someone. "Did ye bribe him with a parrot?"

"No. I made a deal that be against every pirate bone in me body.

But what's done is done. Giuseppe be learning a lot in his profession, and we need that knowledge now."

"What's Giuseppe do? He be a great captain like his dad?" asked Rusty.

The captain shook his head in disappointment. "That's the way it should be. But alas, he be a landlubber."

Rusty was shocked by this, and his face showed it. "Say it ain't so."

"Aye. He be a landlubber." The captain scratched his neck. "If he didn't be making that devastating mistake a few years ago…"

"What be that?" asked Rusty.

"Him choosing to go to college. Now he be a successful finance lad, whatever that be meaning. I don't see him ever coming back to the high seas." He took a drink of his rum. "At least some good be coming from it. He taught me much about growing me treasure, and now he'll be teaching you."

"That be exciting," said Rusty.

Owen rolled his eyes.

"Aye," said the captain. "As ye know, Giuseppe don't be having a favorable view of pirates. I haven't seen me son in years, and I be wantin' to make a good impression on him."

"I always be having a good impression of ya, Captain," said Rusty with a smile.

"Suck up," said Owen under his breath.

"Thanks, Rusty." Captain Dailey wished his son felt the same. As he thought back over his life, he was proud of all he had accomplished. He had succeeded on many adventures and achieved many victories. But now he would trade it all for a good relationship with his son. Guilt bubbled up inside him. He remembered back to when Giuseppe was younger. The captain regretted how he would always choose to go on treasure hunts rather than play Hooking for Apples with his young son. "I'm going to hit the head before he gets here," said the captain as he headed toward the bathroom.

Rusty turned to Owen. "I be lookin' forward to meeting Giuseppe. Captain always be saying good things about him."

"I don't know why," retorted Owen. "I be a better pirate than he could ever be, yet the captain don't be realizing it." Owen fantasized about becoming history's greatest pirate, visualizing himself as a captain one day.

The tavern doors opened, revealing Giuseppe.

CHAPTER THREE

Giuseppe was dressed in traditional pirate attire: white frilly shirt, brown pants, and blue vest. He stood over six feet tall and had dark blonde hair. His blue eyes squinted as he looked around the bar.

It felt strange for him to be back. This environment was so different from the high-tech, fast-paced finance world he was used to now. In this remote part of the country, time seemed to have passed by the pirate community. They still did things the same way they did hundreds of years ago, although some aspects of modern life were starting to infiltrate. He spotted the captain and smiled.

"Welcome," said the captain as he emerged from the back of the tavern. He returned the smile as he walked over and they shook hands.

"Good to see you," said Giuseppe. "I'm glad you finally came to your senses after all these years." He patted the captain on his shoulder.

"Aye," the captain replied, avoiding eye contact. He turned to his crew. "Crew, this here be me son Giuseppe. He be here to teach yar about growing your treasure."

Giuseppe shook his head upon hearing his name. It brought back unpleasant memories that he tried to push from his mind. "You can call me Joey. And nice to meet you all."

The captain pursed his lips upon hearing the name "Joey" but said nothing. "This be Rusty Cannon, our cook and carpenter."

Rusty shot out of his seat and went over to Joey. He shook

Joey's hand excitedly. "Pleasure to meet ya. I be hearing many good things about ya."

"Good to meet you too," said Joey.

"This be Owen Moore, our quartermaster," the captain continued.

Owen remained seated and grunted an acknowledgement.

"And we have one more member of the crew who should be here any minute."

"Okay, great," said Joey. "In the meantime, I have to say that I was surprised when the captain asked me to teach you about personal finance. I don't associate rum-drinking buccaneers with financial literacy. But I have had some great financial teachers in my life, so I feel obligated to return the favor when others are in need of financial knowledge."

"I thought you told the captain you'd never come back," Owen said, unable to restrain himself. "Why haven't you been accepting his other invitations?"

"First," began Joey, "we came to a mutual understanding. He finally agreed to stop doing something he should have stopped doing a long time ago. Isn't that right?" Joey smiled at the captain.

"Aye," the captain said with a half-smile, looking down at the floor.

"And second, this invitation was a lot more appealing than his other invites." Joey remembered being invited to spend two weeks in the middle of a desert, digging for buried treasure that may not have even existed. Then there was the dinner invitation where the only menu items were sun-dried squid and chunky shark's blood stew.

The last member of the crew entered the tavern. Joey's interest perked up.

Sandy stood at the entrance and saw them sitting at the bar. Her thin eyebrows narrowed as she gave a skeptical look. She had gray piercing eyes, a petite nose, and a hard porcelain face. An aura of confidence accompanied her as she walked, with her long chestnut-colored hair bouncing with each step. A brown frock coat hugged her thin frame, and it fell to just above her delicate knees. She was dressed conservatively, but the low-cut white dress hidden beneath the coat gave her a seductive look. "What be going on here?" she scowled.

The captain turned to introduce her. "This be Sandy C. Shore, our master gunner. Sandy, this be me son."

"Hi, I am Joey." He smiled and held out his hand.

"Hi, I don't care," she retorted and walked right by him.

The captain tried to salvage the situation. "Don't mind her," he stammered. "She don't be liking any landlubbers. She thinks everyone should be pirates." He forced a laugh. "But she'll be on good behavior from here on. Won't you now, Sandy?" He shot a glare at her.

"Aye," she said reluctantly.

Motioning to Joey, the captain suggested, "Why don't ya get started."

"Okay, sure." Joey turned to face the crew. "Finance can be pretty boring, so I will try to make this entertaining." He could tell the crew was happy to hear this. "But focus on the financial topics rather than just the entertainment. I will cover eight main lessons, and they can give you the power to achieve financial freedom."

"What be that?" asked Rusty.

"There's no universal definition for financial freedom. It is different for everyone. I encourage each of you to think about what financial freedom means to you."

Rusty nodded.

"I will give you some great tools to help you achieve whatever dreams you may have. You then have a choice. You can either passively listen to these lessons, allowing them to be forgotten over time; or you can take the reins, internalizing these ideas and changing your life. Any questions?"

Rusty looked Joey up and down. "You gonna become a pirate with us and join the crew?"

Confused, Joey responded, "What? Never. I would never live on a ship or associate with pirates. I have a real job on the land. I am just here for a few hours and then I'm gone. In fact, I should be at the office today, but I'm here as a favor to your captain."

Joey wasn't sure where this question came from or what it had to do with achieving financial freedom. Rusty must have already lost interest in trying to improve his financial situation. Not everyone was cut out for being financially free. Some people were content to struggle financially all their lives. "Where did that question come from?"

"You be wearing pirate garb."

"Oh, this thing?" Joey looked at the outfit he was wearing. "My dad had me wear it to make you all feel more comfortable. But I think this shirt looks stupid."

Owen snapped back, "What you be calling stupid?"

Joey looked at his own shirt and realized Owen was wearing the same one but in black. Slightly embarrassed, Joey replied, "Ah, sorry you must have misheard me." He tried to think of something to say as his cheeks got warmer. "Stupendous. That's it. I said this shirt looks stupendous. I like the frills." Joey could tell Owen wasn't buying it.

"What be that necklace you're wearing?" asked Rusty.

"Necklace?" asked Joey. The question confused him again but he was happy to change the topic. He felt around his neck. "Oh this? This isn't a necklace, it's a dog whistle. I was trying to teach my friend's dog new tricks this morning."

"I be loving dogs, except for golden retrievers," said Rusty.

"Why's that?" asked Joey.

"When I be younger, I asked me parents for a golden retriever. But he be a disappointment. Its name be false advertising," Rusty said with a hurt look on his face.

"How so?"

"It never retrieved me any gold."

Joey rolled his eyes.

"Do you have a dog?" asked Rusty, oblivious to Joey's reaction.

"I like goldendoodles, but dogs are expensive. So no, I don't have one. Anyway," Joey said, as he shifted the conversation back to the topic at hand, "the goal for today is to give you general financial advice and answer your specific questions. You are making a lot of mistakes in your financial life that you don't even realize."

Owen declared, "I don't be needin' your advice. I already know about money. I could teach me own class."

Amused, Joey responded, "Oh really? Please, share with us."

"Yar. I know I be needin' to save me money. Spending less be easy."

Joey motioned for him to continue.

"Soap be expensive, so wear the same clothes every day and never shower," Owen said proudly. "As for worrying about debt, don't worry about it. If someone comes looking for ya to pay them back, tell 'em if you ever see 'em again, you're gonna maroon them on an island with lonely Big Bertha and a pooping parrot."

The crew smirked.

"Don't be making fun of this, Owen," warned the captain. "He be coming from far away to help you all, and trust me you need the help."

"I'm not making fun. I be serious." Owen continued with his last point, "If ye be wantin' a life filled with wealth and luxury, you don't need no money for that. Just marry a princess. And if she won't marry you, threaten to feed her to the sharks until she does."

"Terrific advice, thanks for sharing," Joey said sarcastically. "Moving on then, there are a few lessons I would like to share with you."

"Mr. Giuseppe, sir?" said Rusty.

"You can call me Joey. What's your question?"

"With all due respect, I still be in school. Why do I be needing to learn financial lessons when I don't be making much money yet?"

"You are in a terrific position right now. It is important you learn these lessons before you start making a lot of money so you can avoid a lot of the mistakes that your friends will make. Having a strong financial foundation early gives you a tremendous advantage."

"Aye, that be sounding good, matey. I have another question," said Rusty.

Joey shifted in his seat. He wanted to start covering the lessons. The sooner he got through those, the sooner he could be done. He would prefer to be catching up with his dad or be back at work, as opposed to answering Rusty's sometimes bizarre questions.

The captain sensed his frustration. "Save the questions for later. Let him get through his lessons first."

"He's right," said Joey. "I might answer many of your questions in what I have to say. Okay then, the first lesson. Something that will solve a lot of your money problems is this: live below your means." He paused for emphasis.

"Aye, this be a valuable lesson," said the captain.

"Yes. We all know people who spend more than they earn," said Joey.

The crew nodded their heads in agreement. Rusty and Sandy looked at Owen; Owen glared back at them.

Joey wondered if Owen was someone who lived beyond his means. He remembered others who made the same mistake. His neighbor had bought a bigger house than he could afford. His co-workers went out multiple times per week to expensive restaurants, charging it all to credit cards. His cousin had a fancy new car in the driveway but no money in the bank. These people were always stressed about money, trying to make ends meet. Some of them were not even happy. He felt bad for those who went into debt for things that didn't even bring them happiness. "Living below your means is a way to avoid this trap," he said.

"That sounds about as much fun as being flogged with the cat o' nine tails," said Owen.

"There is a misconception that living below your means implies that you can't have fun or own luxurious things. That's not true. The difference is that people in financial trouble buy luxurious things by borrowing money and paying high interest rates. Wealthy people wait until they can actually afford those luxurious items and pay cash."

"Rich people don't be needin' to live below their means, they be rich," protested Owen.

"That's not true either. Even the richest billionaire would be bankrupt if he spent more than he makes. Look at all the famous people and lottery winners who lived beyond their means; making millions a year, but ending up broke. More money is rarely the solution to money problems."

14

The captain nodded in agreement.

Joey continued, "The wealthy absolutely live below their means, or they wouldn't be wealthy. But they look at being able to afford things in a different way. When it comes to something expensive that is out of their budget, rather than thinking how to spend less money, they think of how to make more money. Rather than live within their means, they figure out how to expand their means."

"Listen to that there lesson," said the captain to his crew. "Too many be focusing on spending less, when they should be focusing on making more."

Joey nodded. "The next time you think to yourself 'I can't afford that,' instead ask, 'How can I afford that?' This forces your mind to think of creative ways for how to make more money." He paused for emphasis. He then asked, "What gives you pleasure?"

Rusty perked up. "I be gettin' pleasure from wenches, pillaging, and rum."

"Okay. Do any of you get pleasure from saving money?"

They looked at him with blank faces.

"Learn to get pleasure from saving. Most people think of spending less money as a bad thing. In your mind, redefine pain and pleasure. Start associating pleasure with saving money, and pain with spending money on things you don't need. That will help you accomplish your financial goals."

"Gettin' pleasure from one more thing be sounding good. You can't never have too much pleasure," said Rusty.

The rest of the crew agreed.

Joey adjusted himself on the bar stool and stretched out his back.

The captain noticed and said, "Let's grab us a table." He and Rusty walked to a table in the far corner.

Sandy followed. As she walked by, Joey breathed in her sweet scent of cocoa butter and vanilla. He watched her walk. She had impeccable posture: head up, shoulders back, and chest seeming to lead the way. He felt his heart beating faster as he watched her walk, mesmerized by her hips swaying from side to side.

Joey blinked a few times and shook his head. He got the feeling that Owen was staring at him in anger, but when he turned to look, Owen was looking away from him. They both got up to join the table.

Joey asked the crew with a smile, "Would you like to know the secret to becoming wealthy?"

"Aye!" exclaimed Owen.

Chapter Four

The secret to becoming wealthy isn't about how much you make. It's about how much you save," said Joey. "People who never made over $50,000 a year are now millionaires because they consistently saved and invested. Then there are people who make hundreds of thousands of dollars a year who are in debt up to their eyeballs. Or should I say, eye-patches." Joey smirked at his clever comment.

Owen adjusted his eye-patch and grimaced. "I thought the secret to having lots of treasure be taking risk and having bigger cannon balls than the rest."

"That might help you increase your income, but there is a difference between income and wealth. Just because you make a lot of money doesn't mean you have a lot of money. You measure your income by your paycheck, but your wealth by your net worth. You want to be wealthy enough that you don't have to be stressed about money."

"Not stressed about money? Ha, that be impossible," Owen said under his breath.

"What be net worth?" asked Rusty. "Is that where you catch a rich man in a net?"

"No." Joey couldn't decide if Rusty's comments were annoying or amusing. "You calculate your net worth by adding up all your assets and subtracting your liabilities."

"What be liabilities?" asked Sandy.

Joey was happy to answer her question. Though she hadn't been saying much, she seemed interested in the conversation.

"I know about those," said Rusty before Joey could answer.

Rusty sat up straight and puffed out his chest. He seemed proud to educate his fellow crew on a confusing financial term. "I've done lie-a-bill-a-tease before. That be where you lie all your bills on the floor and they tease you since you can't pay them." He deflated back to his previous sitting position. "It be a horrible feeling, actually."

Not sure how to respond to his comment, Joey continued. "Liabilities is another word for debt. If I were to calculate my net worth, I would add up all my assets such as my savings accounts, home, car, retirement accounts, investments, gold coins etc. Then I would subtract my debt such as my car loan, mortgage, college loan, credit cards, etc. The result is my net worth."

Rusty counted on his fingers. "But my net worth be negative," he said with a sad look on his face.

"That's the case for many young people because of college debt. You just want to make sure that your net worth is consistently increasing. Calculate it every six months to check that it's heading in the right direction."

Rusty nodded.

The captain smiled, seemingly pleased that his crew was learning and asking questions.

"If your net worth is over one million dollars, you can officially call yourself a millionaire," said Joey.

"That's what I be wanting," said Owen.

"And that's what I want for all of you."

Rusty raised his hand.

"Yes," said Joey, acknowledging him.

"You be talking about dollars. What about doubloons?"

"Good question. We use dollars, but you pirates use doubloons. The exchange rate is actually one for one right now, so if you hear me talking about dollars, you can just replace it in your mind with doubloons. Okay." Joey slapped his hands together and looked at the crew. "Who has specific questions?"

"I do," said the bartender from behind the bar. As he stumbled over to them, the goblet of rum in his hand lost half of its contents to the floor. "Do ye want any rum?"

"Aye!" they all yelled in unison.

Joey jumped in his seat, startled by their loud and instant response.

The bartender got up close to the table and leaned over. "What kind do ye want?" His breath filled the air; its putrid stench smelled like a mix of cheap rum, vomit, and rotten oysters.

They all backed away, except for Rusty, who didn't seem to notice the smell. They ordered their preferred drinks and the bartender walked away. They all breathed a sigh of relief.

"Now where were we?" asked Joey.

"Hold on," said Owen. "What be your qualifications? Why should we listen to you?"

"That is a good question. Before you take advice from anyone, you should make sure they know what they're talking about. Oftentimes, acting on bad advice is even worse than getting no advice at all." Joey listed his many qualifications. The crew sat there, seemingly unimpressed.

"Do that be it?" asked Owen, his arms crossed.

Joey was taken aback by this reaction. Clearly, these pirates had high standards. He went on to list even more qualifications. He watched their body language and could tell he wasn't making much of an impression.

Finally, Rusty asked the question that was on all of their minds. "But do yer have any gold?"

"Of course." Joey could feel the tension in the room melt away. They seemed pleased with his response.

The bartender brought over the drinks and sat them down on the table.

In their usual tradition, the captain, Owen, and Rusty banged on the table three times. Then they started singing to the tune of *Row, Row, Row Your Boat*. "Drink, drink, drink your rum; it's the best by far. Drunkily, drunkily, drunkily, drunkily; cheers me mates! Arrrrr!" They smashed their glasses together and each took a big gulp.

Sandy rolled her eyes. "Can we be getting back to the lesson now?"

"Aye, the lesson, the lesson," said the captain. He motioned for Joey to continue.

"Right," said Joey. "I was going to say that gold is not only a diversifier, but it can also protect against inflation, and it is a non-correlated asset."

"And it be shiny!" said Rusty.

Joey smiled. "Yes, and it is shiny." Joey remembered his small treasure chest back in his apartment. He secretly collected gold coins and thought of them shining in the afternoon light. There was something magical about the metal. "Gold can play an important role in a portfolio along with stocks, bonds, cash, commodities, and real estate."

Rusty had a bewildered look on his face. "Now I be more confused than a mermaid in a shoe store."

"Sweet Calypso, that be it!" exclaimed the captain as he jumped out of his chair. He looked at the crew. "I have to go."

"Why?" asked Joey.

The captain seemed unsure how to answer. "I just be needing to check on something, that be all. It won't take but a few minutes. It be great seeing you, Giuseppe. I'll see yer all on the ship." He sprinted off.

"What was that about?" asked Joey.

Sandy replied, "He probably—"

"Looks like even your captain don't want to be hangin' out with ya, you pox-infested scabbies," said Ivan.

Macon laughed. "Yeah, you pox-infested scabbies."

Ivan and Macon were now standing in front of their table. Owen gritted his teeth.

"Let them be, Owen," said Sandy as she put her hand on his shoulder.

"Yeah, listen to the wench. She knows you can't do nothing anyway," said Ivan. He shoved Owen hard enough for him to fall off his seat.

Owen sprang up and drew his sword. His cutlass had a curved blade with a sharp tip.

"Ah, you want to play that way, do ya?" asked Ivan as he pulled out his own cutlass. "Whatcha gonna do now? You wanna be a captain? Ha! The closest you'll ever get is eating a bowl of Captain Crunch, ye sorry excuse for a pirate!"

Outraged that this newbie pirate had the gall to insult his ambitions, Owen lunged forward with his sword. The clank of the blades echoed through the tavern.

Joey and Rusty looked at each other in surprise, not sure what to do.

The bartender continued drinking from his goblet as if nothing out of the ordinary was happening.

Sandy yelled, "Stop! Quit acting like little boys!"

They ignored her plea. Ivan backed up as Owen delivered one blow after another. Realizing that Owen was the better swordfighter, Ivan kicked over the table in front of him to slow Owen down. Owen hopped over the table with ease. Ivan threw a beer bottle at Owen's head, disorienting him. Ivan took advantage of this by rushing forward, delivering his own blows. Owen retreated back toward the bar as he tried to regain his focus. During his retreat, Macon stuck out his foot and Owen tripped over it, making him crash to the ground.

Ivan ran over, stomped his foot on top of Owen's cutlass, and pointed his own sword at Owen's throat.

Owen pulled hard on his own sword to release it from Ivan's foot, but to no avail.

"Leave him alone," said Joey, not sure what else to do. His Excel skills were of no use in this situation.

Ivan chuckled. "Shut up, landlubber, or it will be you next." He turned his attention back to Owen. "Looks like the newbie pirate wins," said Ivan, a big smile on his face. "Admit it, I'm a better pirate than you'll ever be."

"Never!" shouted Owen. He pulled on his cutlass one more time but couldn't release it.

"This be fun," said Ivan, "but not as much fun as I'll be having tomorrow when ye miss your deadline." He emphasized the word "dead." Ivan and Macon laughed.

Wanting to get out from under Ivan, Owen knocked Ivan's

sword away, cutting his own hand in the process. Owen sprang up and ran out of the bar.

"Coward!" shouted Ivan. He and Macon laughed at Owen as they walked back to their table.

Joey, Sandy, and Rusty were still stunned at what happened.

Joey picked up the cutlass and they ran after Owen.

"That's right, you all be cowards!" shouted Macon.

Ivan and Macon cheered each other with their goblets of rum and sat down to gloat over their latest victory.

Chapter Five

Joey ran outside. He felt the afternoon breeze and was relieved to be breathing fresh air again. He shielded his eyes from the sun as he looked for Owen. He saw the ocean washing up against the shore. He looked down the deserted beach dotted with palm trees. He finally saw Owen briskly walking inland toward the town. He ran to catch up. "What happened back there? What deadline are they talking about?"

"I don't want to talk about it," said Owen.

"I grabbed your sword for you." Joey held out the cutlass.

Owen snatched it from him and kept walking.

Sandy and Rusty caught up.

Joey asked Sandy, "Who were those guys?"

"They be two of the crew for Captain Goodman," said Sandy.

"Who is Captain Goodman?" asked Joey.

"The most ruthless pirate to have sailed the seas in many years, dealing death and destruction for no good reason," said Sandy. "Very few be surviving an encounter. Captain Goodman needs to be stopped."

"And I guess Owen doesn't like the crew?" asked Joey.

"Owen don't be likin' most people," said Rusty. "He often be letting his temper get the best of him. But I know what will cheer him up." He shouted to Owen, "Hey, Owen, let's take Giuseppe to the hat store and show him around."

Owen paused before answering, pondering the request. "I don't want to go."

"Oh, come on. He will enjoy seeing the greatest hat store of all time. Plus, he don't be having a hat and doesn't know how to pick one out, ain't that right?"

"That's right. I would have no idea how to pick out a proper pirate hat." Joey preferred to skip the store and get back to the lessons. He didn't want to spend too much time away from the office, but he was curious to see the store.

"See, Owen. Just go for a minute."

Reluctantly, Owen agreed.

"I don't be needing a new hat, so I'll meet you all at the ship with the captain," said Sandy. They said goodbye and she headed off.

They continued toward the hat shop. After a couple of minutes, they walked by a shop with a sign outside that read *Mr. Saylors' Advanced Sailing School. Naval Warfare Training Fit for a Captain.*

"That shop looks interesting. I want to check it out," said Joey.

"No," said Owen hesitantly. "It not be worth the time."

"It will just take a minute." Joey walked to the door and the sign said *Open*. He walked inside.

Mr. Saylors was a heavy older man. He greeted Joey with a rough voice. "Welcome to me sailing school."

"Thanks. I was just walking by with my friends and was intrigued by your shop. What lessons do you offer here?"

"Whatever a captain be needin', we be offering. How can I help?"

Joey saw Owen's head flash in front of the window as he peeked inside.

"Hold your sails," said Mr. Saylors. "Do that be your friend?" He became angry. "I don't be serving his kind. Get out of me shop!" Mr. Saylors ran to the door.

Owen was running away.

Mr. Saylors yelled to Owen, "And if I ever be seeing ye around here again, I'll be grabbing me pistol!"

Joey wondered why he was so upset, but didn't get a chance to ask. Mr. Saylors waved Joey out of the shop and slammed the door behind him. He turned the sign over for it to say *Closed*.

Joey, Owen, and Rusty arrived at the hat shop. It was a stylish shop with brick walls, wooden shelves, and an ornate black ceiling. They had a wide selection of hats, although Joey noticed that many styles were sold out and not re-stocked. The store also sold other items that appealed to pirates.

The salesperson behind the counter greeted them warmly. She was a Korean girl, about five and a half feet tall, with short black hair. Her nametag said *Hope* and she wore a green apron. "Welcome back, Owen," she said.

Owen ignored the greeting and went to the nearest rack. He examined the cut, look, and style of each hat. He tried on the various styles and looked in the mirror, turning from side to side, seeing if the hats fit well with his features. He looked back and forth between the hat and his outfit several times. He seemed at home in the shop.

Joey grabbed a hat and tried it on. He looked in the mirror, copying Owen's movements by turning side to side.

"No," said Owen. "That one be uglier than smashed fish guts thrown on top of a pile of puke. Try this one." He handed Joey a different hat.

Joey tried it on and agreed it looked a lot better.

Rusty grabbed a cart and began shopping. He first grabbed a rather expensive hat without trying it on. He walked to the clothing display, commented that he definitely needed a new outfit, and picked out a velvet crimson vest with matching breeches. The wall of rums from around the world caught his eye. He picked out the mango-flavored rum, then the passion fruit. He looked at the two bottles in his cart, back at the wall, then picked out even more bottles. His cart was filling up quickly and it seemed like he was just getting started.

Joey was surprised at how much Rusty was buying, without giving much thought to his purchases. Curious, Joey asked, "How are you going to pay for all this?"

Rusty smiled as he reached into his pocket. He pulled out a plastic card. "This be a magical device. The salesperson gave it to me last time I be here, and I saved 10% on me purchase. All I do is hand it to her, she swipes it, and I walk out with all me heart's desires."

Joey looked at the credit card and knew how dangerous it could be. "First of all, pirates should be swiping cutlass swords, not credit cards. Secondly, do you know that you have to pay that money back?"

"Of course I be knowing that."

"Do you have the money to pay it back?"

"Not at the moment. But we be expecting some good raids coming up, and that should give me plenty of treasure," Rusty said confidently.

Joey shook his head. He had seen this mistake many times. "That is a common mistake. You anticipate making more money in the future, so you spend like you have already made it. This is how non-wealthy people think."

"What be the problem with that?" Rusty asked.

"A few things. First, there's no guarantee that the extra income will ever become a reality. For landlubbers, bonuses are often smaller than they expect, people back out of commitments, that 'guaranteed' raise turns out not to be guaranteed, etc. For you, those raids may not happen, or they may not be as fruitful as you hope. Don't spend money until it is already in the bank."

"Aye, that happened to me before," Rusty agreed. "I went to a place that was supposed to have never ending treasure. I be digging through bags upon bags, but found nothing."

"What place was that?"

"I think it be called a landfill."

Joey cringed. He was consistently amazed by the things Rusty said. "You went digging through other people's garbage?"

"Aye, but don't you know the expression? 'One man's trash be another man's treasure.' So I dug through piles and piles of their trash, but I found no treasure. The only gold I be finding was some dry crusty gold flakes on some diapers."

Joey scrunched his nose at the thought. He tried to put the

image out of his mind. "Well, lesson learned, I guess. Anyway, the second reason is that it forms a bad habit. If you are always spending money you don't have, once you get any extra money, you have to use it to pay for previous purchases. That makes earning extra money unsatisfying, and it also makes it difficult to build up your savings."

"Is that why I don't be having any treasure?" asked Rusty.

"That's one reason, but I'm sure there are many more. Don't spend like you're already rich; wait for it to actually happen. Otherwise the debt and stress will pile up until it becomes overwhelming."

Rusty now looked stressed. "What should I be doing about it?"

"I have seen people on this path many times before. Luckily for you, it is early enough where we can reverse it. I don't want to see you end up in constant financial pain, or worse yet, bankrupt."

Rusty frowned and his shoulders slumped. "I don't be wantin' to be bankrupt."

"Then the first step is to spend less money than you earn." Joey looked at the many bottles of rum in his cart. They came in different shaped bottles, were various shades of brown, and the labels all had a unique look.

Rusty followed his gaze. "You be wantin' me to spend less on rum? I can't live without rum, matey. I need it every day."

Joey gave him a skeptical look. "You need breakfast every day, not rum."

Rusty looked confused. "But if I stop buying rum, what am I supposed to put on me cereal in the morning?"

"Um, most people put milk on their cereal. You should try it."

"Ah."

"And I'm not saying you have to stop buying rum. Budgeting is about moderation, not elimination. If you want rum in your budget, then put rum in your budget."

Rusty seemed happy he didn't have to stop buying rum.

Joey saw Owen trying on another hat.

Owen whispered to himself, "Now this be a hat fit for a captain." Owen took off the hat and cradled it in his arm like a pet. He walked over to Joey and Rusty. "What be going on here?"

Joey could see he was in a better mood. "I was just about to explain what a budget is."

"What be a budget?" asked Owen.

"It's where you plan ahead of time where your money is going to go."

"People do that?" Rusty seemed surprised by this idea.

"Yes. What do you spend your money on, Rusty?"

"Honestly, I don't know. It be frustrating too. I feel like I should be having more treasure."

"That's common. Many people have no idea what they spend their money on. In order to live below your means, you need to know where you are overspending. That's why keeping a budget is a good idea. It lets you figure out where your money is going, prevents you from over-spending, and most importantly, it makes sure that your biggest priorities are getting funded first."

"What do you be meanin' by that?" asked Owen. "My biggest priority's becoming a captain, the best captain the ocean has ever seen."

"Okay, I'm guessing you need a ship to be a captain?"

Owen nodded.

"Then each time you get a paycheck, you should budget to put aside a certain amount of money for a ship. Do it as soon as you get paid, since that prevents you from wasting your money on less important things. Unallocated money tends to burn a hole in your pocket."

"It does?" Rusty seemed scared and astonished. "It's a good thing I never be having money in me pocket!"

Joey smiled. "It doesn't actually burn a hole in your pocket. That is just an expression."

"Oh," said Rusty.

"What do your budget look like?" asked Owen.

"I actually don't keep a written budget every month."

"You don't?" asked Owen in surprise. "Why should we be taking your advice then?"

"Even though I don't keep a written budget every month, I can tell you where my money is going, and I never spend more than I make. I don't think you should keep a budget forever, either."

"So I don't need a budget then?"

"No, that's not what I said. It is very important that you keep one for a while. Keep a written, detailed budget for at least a few months, until you know where your money is going and you're consistently living below your means. Being in control of your money rather than it being in control of you will make you a happier pirate."

"Aye." Owen nodded his head. He seemed to appreciate this wisdom. "What do you be spending your money on?"

"I spend my discretionary income on—"

"What be discretionary income?" interjected Owen.

"That's the money left over after paying for basic expenses like taxes, food, rent, and clothing. And four-star restaurants, luxury condos, and designer clothes don't count as basic necessities."

Rusty and Owen gave him a confused look.

"Those are things landlubbers enjoy. They will buy expensive clothing and call it a necessity since they have to wear clothing, but that is not correct."

"Do *Pirates of the Caribbean* action figures count as necessities?" asked Rusty.

"No," said Joey. "As for what I spend my discretionary income on, I buy investing courses, career books, instructional videos, I invest in my 401(k), and I give to charity."

Rusty waited for him to say more. "That's it?"

Joey tried to think of what else he spent his money on. Nothing came to mind. "Yup, that's about it."

"What about travel, restaurants, shows, partying, and buying things you want but don't need?"

Joey shook his head. "No, I don't want to waste my money on those things. It's important to save for retirement, consistently increase your income and net worth, and to always be learning and giving back."

"Aye, those be good things, matey. But don't you ever be having some fun?" asked Rusty.

"Fun? Fun isn't going to make me any money or make me any

smarter. Other people can have fun. I am trying to be successful."
Joey turned away and walked to another part of the store.

Rusty and Owen whispered about how they felt Joey was making a mistake, but they didn't want to criticize their teacher. He was free to spend, or not spend, his money in whatever way he wanted.

Chapter Six

Owen showed Joey how to pick out a stylish pirate hat. He explained how to pick a hat based on the shape of his face and the colors of his outfit. Joey tried on a brown tri-cornered hat that everyone liked.

"That one be looking good," said Owen. "You should buy it."

"No, I don't need it. I only buy necessities," Joey reminded him.

"Aye," Owen said as he lowered his head. He walked over to the spices shelf. It had a dozen different spices on display, each one finely-ground in its own bowl. He reached for the spoon in the garlic powder bowl. He mixed the white powder around, watching the individual crystals fall from the spoon. He enjoyed the scent. He put the spoon back and went to the cinnamon bowl. He smiled as he brought the spice to his nose and smelled its aroma. He did the same with the rosemary.

"Are you a cooking fan?" asked Joey.

"Aye. When you're on the ocean for days at a time, good spices can add a lot to bland food." Owen walked to the register to buy the hat he was holding.

Hope smiled at him as he approached the counter. "How have you been, Owen?"

"Fine, thanks."

"You only need one hat today?"

Owen glanced at Joey then turned back to the clerk. "Aye." He reached in his pouch and pulled out a few doubloons. He looked at the hat, back at Joey, and back at the clerk. "Actually, I be having enough hats. I don't be needing this one today." He pushed the hat away.

"Really?" she asked, surprised. "That's the first time I've ever seen you say no to a hat!"

Owen scratched his neck. "Aye." He walked away from the counter.

Rusty brought over his cart to check out. It was much less full than before. After talking to Joey, he had taken the time to decide what he needed versus what he just wanted. After thinking about some of the items he had picked, he realized he didn't even want some of them. They were impulse buys that he would have regretted later.

Hope greeted Rusty and asked, "Did you find everything you wanted today, sir?"

"Aye, more than I needed," said Rusty with a laugh.

She rang up his items. "Your total is fifty-seven doubloons. Would you like to donate some money to the local homeless shelter?"

"Naw," said Rusty as he shook his head. "I don't be having no treasure to donate yet. If I ever be finding Duarte's map I'll be sure to donate though," he laughed.

"Ha, good luck with that," said Joey. "If you want to waste half your life searching for a fairy tale, go right ahead."

"You be knowing about Duarte's map?" asked Rusty.

"Of course. The great Captain Duarte," Joey said with sarcasm. "How he accumulated more gold, silver, and treasure than any other pirate this century. How there is a map that leads to a fortune almost as big as the buried treasure of Blackbeard. How there is a mystical riddle that gives clues to its location. Blah, blah, blah. I hate that map and I hate that legend." He was becoming angry. "Do you know why?"

Rusty shook his head.

"Because none of it's true," Joey said, slamming his fist on the counter. "I love gold and hidden treasure as much as you. But the whole thing is a myth and I won't have anything to do with it. The captain spent decades trying to find that riddle, and it ruined our relationship. Luckily he's come to his senses and is done with that now. That's the only reason I came back, because he agreed to stop looking for it."

Rusty and Owen looked at each other. Owen began to speak but stopped himself.

"Aye," said Rusty, not sure what else to say.

"Now let's get back to more important issues, such as your charity comment. How much did you spend today?" asked Joey.

"Fifty-seven doubloons."

"And you can't spare one or two doubloons for charity?"

Rusty thought about this. "But I be wanting to make a big difference when I donate. One or two doubloons ain't gonna do much, matey."

"One or two doubloons might be able to feed a starving child for a whole day. You just don't know. Some charities get businesses and others to match your donation, so your doubloons could go farther than you think. Giving to charity may not make you richer, but it will give you a richer life."

Rusty said, "I be too young to give to charity."

"You're never too young to donate. When I was a kid, my allowance went into three jars: one for saving, one for spending, and one for giving away. I believe that the way you act now with small amounts of money will be the same way you act when you have large amounts of money. It is important to get into the habit as early as you can, even if it is just donating a dollar per month."

"He be right," said Owen. "I be giving to charity all the time."

This surprised Joey. "That's good to hear, Owen. I'm proud of you. Do you get an inner satisfaction when helping those less fortunate in your community?"

Owen chuckled. "No, me hearty. That's not why I be donating. I be a selfish pirate. I care about me treasure chest filling up faster, and giving to charity helps with that."

Joey looked disgusted.

Owen continued, "Everybody knows the more ye give, the more ye get. There be some mystical force when you be giving away treasure. Treasure goes out one door and more treasure comes in another door. I think the secret to being rich be simple: give more and more will come back to yar."

This kind of talk angered Joey. He took a deep breath and tried to speak calmly. "While there is truth to that, that's the wrong way to look at charitable giving." He thought for a second. "Owen, there must be one cause you are passionate about."

"Aye, there be one cause."

"What's that?"

"Times be tough for a lot of pirates, and many of them can't afford any rum. That's why I be supporting the AARP."

Joey definitely didn't expect this answer. "You support The American Association of Retired Persons?"

"What be that? No, The Alliance Against Rum-less Pirates. The fact that there are pirates sailing out on the high seas without any rum be a devastation and must be stopped."

"Right, thanks for sharing." Joey turned back to Rusty, staring silently.

"Argh. You be right." Rusty gave three doubloons to the charity fund at the register.

Hope smiled. "Thank you."

They started to leave the store. As he walked toward the entrance, Joey heard someone sobbing in the back room. He walked to the noise and opened the door. On the floor, he saw a girl there crying. She was wearing a green apron, and her nametag said *Misty*. He rushed over and asked, "What's wrong?"

"Oh nothing," she said. "I'm fine."

Hope came running over. "What's wrong?" She sat down next to Misty and brushed through her hair.

"Oh nothing," Misty said. "I just be hearing you all talk about money, and it makes me sad."

"Why's that?" asked Joey.

"Because I'm twenty-seven years old, and I'm a college graduate. I wanted to be so much more successful by now. But my money problems keep getting worse, not better. It seems like nothing is ever going to change. It's hopeless."

"Whoa, hold on there," said Joey. "I know a lot about finance.

In fact I have been teaching personal finance lessons all day. Maybe the lessons can help you too."

"I doubt it. I live paycheck to paycheck. They wouldn't apply to me."

Joey shook his head. "That's not true at all. These lessons apply to everyone."

Rusty and Owen came in to look at what was going on.

Misty lowered her head. "Financial lessons are just theoretical; they don't actually help anyone in the real world."

"That comment would come as a shock to a lot of people. There are hundreds of ordinary people who blog about how they went from living paycheck to paycheck to being financially free."

She dabbed her eyes with a tissue. "Really? What do they say?"

"They all have their own stories and I encourage you to look them up. But in general, they followed the same five steps."

Her eyes lit up with interest. "Can you tell me the steps?"

Chapter Seven

"Step one, change your mindset," said Joey. "These people had been going along, accepting their fate of being poor for the rest of their lives. But then one day they snapped. They felt tired of being financially stressed. They were fed up with having no money in the bank. They became angry at their credit card debt. They stood up and said, 'I'm not going to take it anymore.' They decided to change, and they never looked back."

"How did they do it?" Misty asked, her eyes open wide with excitement.

"They did step two, which is cut expenses. They listed every expense they had. Then they cut the fat, sometimes dramatically if that's what it took. They basically made a budget."

"I can cut some expenses," she said, her confidence rising. "What did they do next?"

"They started saving every dollar they could. They paid themselves first. When they cut their expenses, they saved the difference."

Her body posture improved. "I have been meaning to save more. I even have a savings account I could use."

"That's great," Joey said. "Then you can do step four, which is increase your income."

She rolled her eyes and looked discouraged again. "I knew there was a catch. Sure, it's easy to say I should make more money. But I don't have any idea how."

"Oh really? How many days have you spent researching new

ways to make money?"

She stared back at him in surprise. "Um, zero," she muttered.

"Well, that's your first problem. There are lots of ways to increase your income. Do an Internet search on ways to do it. Go to the library to read books on the topic. Learn new skills to get a better job. Become an entrepreneur, which can be as simple as starting a dog walking company."

"That's a good point," she said. "I've always wanted to make more money, but I've never looked into how to do it. I should do that."

"Yes, absolutely. But it won't be easy. That's where the fifth step comes in."

"What's that?"

"Never give up. Becoming financially free can be hard. It takes sacrifice; you will fail at times. But you never truly fail until you give up on yourself. Ask any super-successful person if they made mistakes and failed along the way, and every one of them will say yes. The difference is they didn't give up. Just know that many other people have risen above living paycheck to paycheck, and you can too."

She nodded but had a skeptical look on her face. "I'm sure you're right, but those people had better jobs. I just make minimum wage."

"Apparently you haven't heard of Jen Smith. She is known as the Millionaire Mommy Next Door. She went from earning minimum wage as a donut and coffee waitress working the graveyard shift to becoming a self-made millionaire by age forty. There are countless inspirational rags to riches stories. Go find them and copy their examples."

"Wow. I had no idea. Thank you so much!"

"My pleasure."

"That was fascinating," said Hope. "You have me thinking even I can improve my finances."

"You can," said Joey.

They all stood up and walked out to the front of the store.

"Yeah, but I don't know," said Hope.

"Why not?" asked Joey.

"I like your advice. But..."

"But what?"

"What will my friends think? If I spend less money and stop going out with them as much, won't they think less of me?"

Joey nodded. "My friend had the same thought. She lived in San Francisco and figured spending hundreds of dollars a month on social activities was just the normal thing to do. But she wanted to get out of the financial rat race. She was nervous about what her friends would say, so she delayed making any changes. She imagined she would have to sit at home alone every weekend while her friends partied. A few weeks went by. One night her friend asked her to go out for a fancy dinner as usual. She decided this was her time. Feeling nervous, she courageously told her friend that she couldn't go to dinner because she was trying to save money. Then she held her breath."

"What happened?" Hope asked excitedly.

"To her surprise, her friend said 'Me too!' It turns out many of her friends wanted to save money. She did some research into all the free activities they could do together in the city, and it turned out there were a lot. Now she and her friends go out every weekend and have a lot of fun, but spend very little money."

"Really? I never would have guessed. Maybe my friends want to do free things too."

"Maybe. You never know. Your friends can be powerful allies on your road to success. Telling your friends that you have the goal of becoming financially free can be one of the best things you can do."

"Why?" she asked, a skeptical look on her face.

"If you tell all your friends about a goal you have, you know they're going to ask you how it's going. You don't want to tell them that you gave up on it, so that kind of peer pressure can be a powerful motivator. Another point is that your friends want to see you succeed, so they might offer you help or advice that you wouldn't have received otherwise. Or a few of your friends might have the same goals, so you could form an accountability group. Having accountability partners has been shown to increase the chance of success."

"Those are good points. I can see where telling all your friends is a good idea. I may even inspire a few of them to improve their own finances."

A man emerged from the back room. "Well, if it isn't my best customer. How ya doing, Owen? And Rusty's here too. Must be me lucky day." He was middle-aged with an Australian accent. He dressed sharply but casually, and had a big smile on his face.

"Oliver!" shouted Rusty happily.

"You mates causing trouble out here?" asked Oliver.

"Doing our best to," said Owen, smiling.

Oliver looked at Joey. "And who might this dashing young fellow be?"

Rusty introduced them. "Giuseppe, this be Oliver Fosters. Giuseppe, this be Oliver."

Joey extended his hand. "You can call me Joey. Nice to meet you."

"Likewise," smiled Oliver.

"Oliver be the owner of the shop here," said Rusty.

"Oh really?" asked Joey.

"Yes, mate," said Oliver.

"He be owning a couple dozen other hat stores around the world," Rusty said.

"A multi-national corporation, huh? Impressive," said Joey. "How's business?"

"Business is great. The hats are really popular; I can't keep up with demand. Look at my shelves, they're half empty."

"Sounds like you need to fire your hat supplier and get a new one," Joey commented.

Oliver chuckled. "Then I would have to fire myself. My employees and I make them all ourselves."

"Really?" Joey, Owen, and Rusty all asked at the same time.

"Yeah, I have an old factory where I make them down the road."

"Can we be seeing it?" asked Owen.

"Sure. You want to see it now?"

"Aye!" Owen and Rusty followed Oliver out of the shop.

Joey paused. He felt like they should go back to the ship, but he liked learning about new businesses. He decided to follow the others. Misty and Hope waved goodbye and thanked him for his help.

⚔   ⚔   ⚔

As they were walking, Joey asked Rusty, "I forgot to look when you checked out. How did you pay for your items today?"

"Me credit card, of course," said Rusty.

"You shouldn't be spending money you don't have. It's really hard to break that habit."

"It only be fifty-seven doubloons."

"Charging fifty-seven doubloons isn't a big deal at first, but then one day you wake up thousands of doubloons in debt. And you have to pay over seventeen percent interest on it."

Rusty thought about his comment. "You know, I already be surprised by how much I've charged in a short amount of time. But I don't know what to do. I tried to stop but can't."

"Yes, and it will only get harder. Here is what I want you to do." Joey motioned for Owen to come over. "The first step to breaking the habit is to stop carrying around your credit cards. I want you to only pay with cash. So take out your credit cards and give them to Owen."

"Huh?" asked Rusty.

Oliver overheard their discussion. "That be good advice. Stop carrying those cards around so you aren't tempted to use them for an impulse buy. Give them to someone you trust."

"I'm guessing you trust your crewmate Owen, right?" Joey asked to Rusty.

Rusty frowned at Owen. "I guess so."

"Don't worry, he won't spend on them. He's just preventing you from charging on them for a while."

Rusty pursed his lips and stomped his foot on the ground. "Do I have to?"

"Yes. The first step is to stop spending more than you make."

Rusty grabbed his credit cards and reluctantly gave them to

Owen. Afterward, he felt like a piece of himself had died.

"Good job. Now Owen, do not give them back to Rusty unless he really, really needs them. If he does need one back, he has to tell you why he needs it, and you get to flog him."

Rusty went from feeling sad to fearful. "Flog me?"

Owen smiled. "I be liking this." He thought about it further. "But if we really want to discourage him, we should keelhaul him."

Rusty's eyes opened wide in fear. "No, not that!"

"What's keelhaul?" asked Joey.

"It be a horrible form of punishment. Captain Goodman uses it to instill fear in enemies, and even the crew," said Owen.

"That sounds pretty harsh. I thought the punishment was rough at my job, but keelhauling sounds a lot worse. I think a light flogging sounds just fine."

Rusty breathed a sigh of relief.

"What kind of job you be doing?" asked Owen.

"I come up with investment ideas, so I do research on stocks and bonds and other asset classes."

"Stocks and bonds?" asked Rusty. "I be hearing of those before. They sound exciting, but I don't know anything about them."

"Yeah, most people don't. A lot of people think stocks and bonds are these magical things that go up and down for no reason. But there are real companies behind them."

"Where do stocks and bonds come from?" Rusty asked it in a way that reminded Joey of a child asking his parents where babies come from.

"Well, when an investor and a company love each other very much..." Joey chuckled to himself.

Rusty and Owen looked at him with blank faces.

"Never mind," said Joey, disappointed they didn't find his joke funny.

"I don't be caring about where they come from," complained Owen. "How can I make money with them?"

"Well, Rusty had a good question. There are lots of ways to make money in the market. But it's a little premature to talk about that if

41

you don't even know what stocks and bonds are or why they exist in the first place."

Oliver stopped walking. "Here's the factory."

In front of them they saw a very large, old building that looked like a warehouse. They entered, and Joey was shocked by what he saw.

Chapter Eight

The captain's quarters were on the lower level of the ship. It was a spacious room and the circular windows gave a nice view of the ocean. Oriental rugs covered the wooden floor. Books of all types filled the large mahogany bookcase. Maps from around the world hung on the wall. In the corner of the room was a majestic bed sitting next to a dresser. The room was well-kept except for the disorganized desk where the captain was sitting, which had books and articles scattered across it.

Captain Dailey sat hunched over a book. Rusty's comment had triggered an idea, and he was furiously flipping through the pages to confirm it. He came to a passage and read it for probably the hundredth time. This time, however, it made more sense. After so many years, he felt like he was finally making progress.

He returned Duarte's biography to the bookshelf and smiled.

⚔ ⚔ ⚔

Joey looked around the large room where over one hundred people were working. The dingy facility clearly hadn't been renovated in years, if not decades. The conveyor belt filled with hats looked rusty as it cranked along slowly. The wooden storage units seemed to be rotting. Paint was peeling from the walls, the floor looked like it had been there for a century, and some of the machines were held together with duct tape.

"This is it," said Oliver. "Not much to look at."

Joey stood there, appalled. "Those machines are making your products? I'm shocked they haven't fallen apart by now. Were they even designed to make hats?"

"Ha, not at all. This was the only factory I could afford at the time, so I retrofitted all the machinery for my purposes."

Joey shook his head. "A company of your size should have much better facilities. Why don't you build a new factory?"

"A new factory? Do you know how much that would cost? I don't have that kind of money."

"If you have a profitable and growing business, there many ways to finance a new factory. Do you know one of the main ways?"

Owen answered, "Pillage someone else's factory."

"Um, clever idea, but that's not legal." Joey turned back to Oliver. "You could access the capital markets."

"Huh?" replied Oliver.

"In other words, you could issue debt or equity to raise capital."

"Huh?"

"You know, stocks and bonds?"

"That sounds pretty complicated. How would that work?"

Joey smiled. "Rusty, you know how you wanted to know where stocks and bonds came from? Here's your chance to learn."

Rusty's ears perked up.

"I don't know," said Oliver. "That sounds pretty fancy for a simple hat maker like myself. Why don't I just go to the bank to get a loan?"

"You could do that, but you are a large business, so going to a bank would be expensive, slow, and restrictive. A better option is to issue bonds."

"What are those?"

"A bond is like an IOU. An investor lends your company $10,000 and in return gets a bond, which is basically a contract on a piece of paper. Since he is a bondholder, the company pays him 5% interest per year, so one bond pays $500 per year. After ten years, your company pays the investor back his original $10,000. When the investor gets his money back, that is referred to as the bond maturing."

"But $10,000 isn't enough for a factory," objected Oliver.

"Your company would do this with many investors. You could raise millions of dollars for the new factory if you issue enough bonds."

"I be wanting to buy those bonds," said Owen. "That be sounding like an easy way to make 5% a year."

"That's true," said Joey, "but there is still risk. His company could go bankrupt before it pays back your bond. If it does, then you'd get back less than your original $10,000 investment."

"I don't want to be taking risk. What be a risk-free investment?" asked Rusty.

"There's no such thing as a completely risk-free investment. But generally speaking, the bonds of the US government are considered to be risk free. These are called Treasury bonds."

"If Treasuries be risk-free, why would anybody invest in other kinds of bonds?" asked Oliver.

"Good question. That's because US Treasury bonds pay less interest than other bonds. For example a US Treasury bond might pay 3% interest per year, whereas a high-risk bond could pay 6% interest per year."

Oliver nodded.

"So bonds are one way your company could raise money for the new factory," said Joey. "Another option is to issue stock."

"Stock?" asked Owen. "Like the stock of alcohol I be storin' below the ship's deck?"

Rusty got excited and started to drool. "You be having a stock of alcohol below deck?"

Owen regretted saying anything. He mumbled to himself, "Argh, I should have kept me blowhole shut." He then looked directly in Rusty's eyes and said, "If ye touch it, you'll be meat for the sharks."

Rusty lowered his head like a scolded puppy. He was sure to never go looking for the secret stash of rum.

Joey ignored their conversation. "An advantage of issuing stock is that you never need to pay that money back."

"I'm liking this stock idea," said Oliver, smiling.

They heard a screeching sound coming from a machine, and then smoke began to rise. One of the employees ran over with a bucket of water, splashing it on the machine. He grabbed some tools from his belt and began tinkering. He then waved the all clear, signaling everything was fine.

Joey shook his head, then continued speaking to Oliver. "Yes, but raising money by issuing stock has drawbacks. Stockholders are part owners of the company, so you have to give them part of the profit forever."

"Forever?" asked Oliver.

"Yes. So if you grow this into a huge company, your stock investors will become rich right alongside you. That's assuming your company doesn't go bankrupt, of course."

"Let's hope that doesn't happen!"

"Agreed. Stocks are riskier than bonds, so the potential rewards are greater with stocks. With a bond, the most an investor can earn is the interest paid. But with a stock, the investor has unlimited upside potential."

"What if the investor wants to sell his stock?"

"He can sell it to someone else using a stock market. On the stock market, you can buy and sell shares of companies throughout the world."

"How much treasure could he sell the stock for?" asked Rusty.

"The prices of stocks move everyday based on whether people think the company will be more or less profitable in the future. For example, if your company issues a press release saying demand for your hats is up, your stock price will probably increase. But if you issue a statement saying that your competitor is taking away your customers due to lower prices, your stock price would probably go down. There are people who spend most of their life trying to predict which stocks are going to go up and down."

"That be sounding boring. I'd rather stick a hook in me eye," said Owen.

"It's actually very exciting for the people who are good at it. If you're exceptionally talented, you can become a billionaire."

Owen was focused on becoming a millionaire; he couldn't even comprehend how much money a billionaire must have.

Joey continued, "Peter Lynch was a great investor who had a return of 2,500% while managing his fund. That was five times more than the return of the market. But even great stock pickers have fears and concerns. What do you think? What was Peter's greatest fear?"

"Captain Hook!" exclaimed Rusty.

"No, wrong Peter. We are talking about Peter Lynch. What was Lynch's worst enemy?"

"A rope," said Owen, smirking.

"I didn't say 'lynching.'" Joey exhaled in frustration. "Never mind, I will just tell you. A stock investor's greatest fear is that the stocks of the companies he owns will go bankrupt. If a company goes bankrupt, it usually means its stock goes to zero. And that violates Warren Buffett's rules."

"Who is Warren Buffett?" asked Oliver.

A crashing sound came from the corner of the room. A rickety wooden storage shelf had broken in two, causing the heavy supplies to crash to the floor. Two employees ran over with brooms and mops to clean up the mess.

"Warren Buffett is one of my heroes. Known as the 'Oracle of Omaha,' he's one of the richest men on the planet and one of the greatest investors ever. When it comes to investing, he has two rules. Rule number one: don't lose money. Rule number two: don't forget rule number one."

"Those be some simple rules," said Owen.

"Sometimes simplicity is the best policy."

"I have a question," said Rusty. "You said if I own stock, then I be an owner of the company. Since I be an owner, can I make whatever rules me want? Can I make the company buy me a ship? And force everyone to dress like a pirate?"

Joey imagined an office full of accountants, finance nerds, and corporate executives, all dressed in pirate attire and eye patches. "It's true you are a partial owner of the company, but a very small partial owner. There could be millions of other partial owners, so unfortunately you can't tell the company to do whatever you want."

"I can't do anything, even though I be an owner?"

"I didn't say that. You still have power as a shareholder, even if you only have a few shares."

"Like what?" asked Oliver.

"You can vote on important shareholder issues, such as who should be on the board of directors, or if they should buy a different company. You can submit a resolution where you suggest the company change something, and all the other shareholders vote on your idea."

"Really?" Oliver thought of a few things he would like changed at popular companies.

"Yes. You can go to the annual shareholder meeting and ask management questions in person. You get access to the company's financial information. They send you annual reports, which give updates on the business and tell you the direction they are taking the company. You receive any cash dividends the company pays out."

"That be quite a lot."

Joey nodded. "Shareholders have many rights, but most people don't realize it."

A loud bang startled them. Suddenly the conveyor belt stopped moving.

Oliver grunted. "I need to go fix this." He turned to Joey. "I think you be right. Probably time to upgrade this factory."

"Yeah, I agree." Joey looked at his watch. "We should probably get going. Thanks for the tour. You make a high-quality product."

"Thanks, mate."

They said good-bye and left the factory.

CHAPTER NINE

They left the factory and started walking back to the ship.

"I be liking Oliver," said Rusty. "He be fun, and he works hard."

"We be knowing about that," said Owen.

"You guys have to work hard on the ship?" asked Joey.

"Aye, especially since the captain fired a crewmember a while back," said Owen.

"He did? Why doesn't he hire somebody new?" Joey asked.

"Because the pirate community be shrinking. Too many people be becoming landlubbers, so he can't recruit anyone."

"That's too bad he had to fire someone. What's that person up to now?" asked Joey.

Rusty and Owen gave each other an uncomfortable glance.

Joey felt the tension rise. He decided to drop the topic. "What's that up there?"

In the distance they saw a man in a cage. They walked up to him.

"What you be doing in there?" asked Rusty. "You playing a game?"

"Do this be looking like a game?" the man asked angrily. He was very thin; it looked like he hadn't eaten in weeks. He had a metal hook for a hand, which showed from underneath his brown shirt. He was losing his hair and was covered in scars. He walked back and forth on his peg leg.

"Why are you in there?" asked Joey.

"As a punishment. Why do you care?"

"What happened?" asked Owen.

"What happened was I took a loan from Captain Goodman, and I be late paying it back."

"Oh, sorry to hear that," said Joey. "I haven't heard good things about Captain Goodman, probably charges really high late fees."

"Aye, be charging an arm and a leg."

"I'm sure," said Joey.

"No," said the man. "You don't be understanding. An arm and a leg!" He shook his hook and peg leg.

"Ouch!" said Rusty.

"Now I be trapped in this cage, starving. Supposed to be a lesson to others. I'm afraid I be a dead man." He looked away, his eyes full of sadness. "But you better get going. If they catch me talking to anyone for too long, they bring out the torture devices."

Joey cringed. Owen walked away; he seemed very disturbed.

"Alright," said Joey. "Sorry to hear about your troubles. I hope it all turns out okay."

The man didn't respond but stood there in silence, looking off far into the distance.

After a long walk, they finally saw the ship in the distance. It was a grand ship named the *Prosperous Guardian*. It rocked majestically on the ocean waters, lit up by the bright afternoon sun. The ship's white sails flapped in the breeze.

As they got closer, it became clear that it had seen its fair share of battles. Some of the wood was damaged by cannon fire. There was a hole in the side, patched with wooden planks.

They boarded the ship. Joey looked around for the captain but didn't see him.

Sandy walked over. "Where have you guys been?" she asked, sounding irritated.

"We be seeing the pirate hat factory," said Owen with a subtle smile.

"Really?" she asked.

"Aye. And then we be learning about stocks and bonds," said Rusty.

"Stocks and bonds?"

"Aye. Stocks be ownership in a company, and bonds be paying you interest until the bond reaches its maturity," said Rusty.

Joey looked at Rusty, surprised and impressed that he was able to articulate what he had learned.

"I've heard of stocks and bonds before." said Sandy. "Actually, do you know the difference between a bond and a man?"

Joey had studied a lot about finance, and even earned the prestigious Chartered Financial Analyst designation. But he had never heard of a correlation between a bond and a man. "No, what is the difference?"

"A bond matures." Sandy laughed.

The male crew didn't find it funny.

"Right..." said Joey, disappointed. He looked around for the captain.

"Giuseppe, why didn't you wait for me before teaching stuff?" asked Sandy. "I like learning."

"You can call me Joey, and—"

"Why do the captain be calling you Giuseppe if your name be Joey?" she asked.

"He doesn't think Joey is a worthy pirate name, so he calls me Giuseppe." Joey remembered being made fun of growing up for having the pirate name. They were memories he often tried to forget. "But I refuse to go by that name. My name is Joey."

"Well, Joey, don't be teaching these barnacle brains anything without me," she said.

"I'm happy to teach. What finance questions do you have?"

Sandy took a deep breath. An issue had been on her mind for weeks now, and she hoped he could address it. "You seem to know what you be talking about. I've been stressed with an issue lately. Maybe you can help. If not, you'll be walking the plank."

Joey couldn't tell if she was kidding or not.

"It be a pirate's life for me, and I want it to be that way forever. I be working hard, harder than any of these blokes." The crew laughed at this until they realized she was serious. "But when I get too old for working this hard, I still want me independence and freedom. I want to sail to any sandy seashore me want, either to relax on it or conquer it. I wanna rely on meself, not on any man to take care of me. I chew up and spit out men for breakfast."

"Wow, we have a feisty one here. I like it," said Joey. "So, Sandy, it sounds like you want a plan to save for retirement. I can help you with that. But it isn't easy. Are you ready for a challenge?"

She didn't have to think about her answer. "I live for challenge."

"Okay good, because it is worth it. Retirement is ultimate financial freedom. You can do whatever you want, whenever you want. It's where you have enough money saved so you can just live off the interest. That's the dream."

Sandy nodded, seeming to picture her dream retirement.

"Unfortunately, most people don't achieve this dream. They struggled financially during their working years, and didn't save much money. Now they don't have enough retirement savings, so they struggle financially during retirement. Imagine working for someone else all your life and not having anything to show for it at the end."

This thought made Sandy even more determined to get her financial life in order. "That's not gonna be me. I take control of me own life. I just be needin' to figure out the steps."

"Well, today is your lucky day. I will show you the steps. Most people don't realize that they need to be responsible for their own retirement. Pensions are going away, and there's a chance Social Security could be broke by the time young people need it."

She wasn't sure what Social Security was, but felt it didn't sound like a good situation.

"Even if Social Security is around, don't expect to live a lavish lifestyle with that money. People who only have Social Security as a source of income often have a much lower standard of living than when they were working."

"How do those people be paying for unexpected expenses?"

"It depends. Sometimes if their car breaks down or they have a medical expense, many of those people have to rely on their children or other family members for money. Just think of spending your last years on Earth begging your children for money, since you weren't responsible enough to plan for your own future."

"I'm gonna be the best mother ever," she snapped. The thought of being in that situation was unthinkable. "I'm gonna take care of me kids, not make them take care of me." Now she really wanted to know how to fix her current financial situation. "Come on already, tell me the steps."

"Boy, she's so demanding. Note to self, do not date this girl," said Joey.

Owen and Rusty laughed.

"What did you say?" demanded Sandy. She crossed her arms.

"Nothing," said Joey, smiling.

"Lots of guys want me. You would be lucky to date me."

"Please. First of all, you couldn't handle me," Joey said smiling. "Second, what makes you think you're better than other girls anyway?"

She thought about it for a second, then said, "None of your business. That's just the way it be."

"Okay, your highness." Joey rolled his eyes and continued the explanation. "There are three important factors that will determine how your retirement will look. The first is how early you start saving. The second is how much you save. The third is how long you wait to retire."

Sandy had calmed down and was listening intently. Her arms were no longer crossed. "Me pirate lads aren't saving for their golden years yet. They say I be having plenty of time."

"Do your pirate lads have lots of treasure?" asked Joey.

She laughed. "They don't have no treasure, they be borrowing treasure from me. Then when they don't pay me back I make them scrub the poop deck."

"Here's a tip: don't take financial advice from broke people." He remembered seeing an article saying that half of Americans aren't saving a penny for retirement. The article went on to say that most people rank home remodeling and vacation as higher priorities. "Usually following the crowd when it comes to money is a bad idea.

If all your friends jumped off the plank, would you?"

"Ha, no," said Sandy.

"Saving for retirement can be tough, especially when fighting against two powerful enemies."

Owen became tense and looked around. "Show me the enemies and I'll show 'em me blade."

"I don't think your cutlass will do any good against these enemies," said Joey.

"I bet it will!" Owen exclaimed as he drew his sword, spinning around to look for the opponents.

"We'll see. The first enemy is inflation."

"Inflation?" Owen looked perplexed as he put away his cutlass.

"I be knowing that," said Rusty. "The other day I saw a kid with a circular plastic inflation. He tried to attach it to the back of our ship with a rope to ride the waves."

Joey smirked. He was starting to find Rusty's bizarre comments amusing. "No, that's an inflatable tube. Inflation is how things tend to cost more over time. For example, about seventy years ago you could go see a movie and get popcorn for one dollar. You could buy a Hershey bar for ten cents about fifty years ago. And twenty years ago gasoline was less than one dollar per gallon."

Owen said, "I've never been to a movie, bought a Hershey bar, or driven a car. What does that have to do with us?"

Joey tried to put the concept into pirate terms. "How much does a bottle of rum cost today?"

"Twenty doubloons," said Owen.

"In forty years, assuming a modest 2% annual inflation rate, that same bottle of rum will cost more than forty doubloons."

Owen got upset that something he had never heard of would make his rum more expensive. "Argh, inflation. I'll cleave it to the brisket!"

Sandy was not happy discovering that more challenges stood in her way to financial freedom. "What be the other enemy?"

"Taxes. They take away money from your paycheck, which makes it harder to save, and they eat away your investment returns over time." He paused. "But there is a way to avoid taxes for decades to come."

"Don't be thinking such stupid thoughts," she said. "Everybody knows the tax man be getting his take, no matter what. The captain learned that the hard way."

Joey looked around the ship for the captain. "Where is he anyway? And why did he run out of the tavern so quickly?"

Sandy shrugged her shoulders. "He's probably down in his quarters trying to find Duarte's treasure."

Rusty and Owen looked at each other.

Joey felt anger bubbling up inside him. "What did you say?" he demanded.

"Captain Duarte Bonaventura, he be the most famous pirate of recent history. He accumulated—"

Joey cut her off mid-sentence. "I know who he was, or supposedly was," he growled. "Why is the captain still looking for that riddle?"

"Because he always be looking for it." She made it sound like this answer was obvious.

Rusty and Owen lowered their heads and backed away.

Joey felt blood and adrenaline pumping through his veins. He clenched his fists. "He told me he stopped looking for that stupid myth a long time ago. Are you saying that's not true?"

Sandy gave him attitude back. "Do I look like his assistant? I don't know what he's been up to today. Go ask him yourself."

Joey clenched his jaw in anger. How could he be so stupid? Of course the captain wouldn't stop looking for that cursed object. He couldn't; it was an addiction. Joey stomped over to the stairs and then skipped down two steps at a time. He walked to the captain's quarters and slammed open the door.

CHAPTER TEN

The captain looked up in surprise.

Joey saw him reading a book. He recognized it instantly as Duarte's biography. "You told me you stopped looking for that stupid riddle!" he yelled, his face turning red.

"I did," said the captain calmly as he pushed his seat back away from Joey.

"You're looking for it right now; I caught you red-handed! You're looking in that stupid biography again, and even Sandy admitted you were searching for it." He paced back and forth. "The only reason I came here is because you said you were done with that wild goose chase. That treasure ruined my childhood, and I'm not going to let it ruin my adulthood."

Rusty, Owen, and Sandy tiptoed down the stairs to eavesdrop on the argument.

"I intended to stop looking for the treasure," said the captain. "But Rusty's comment got me thinking. Then I figured out a piece of the puzzle. I be close to finding it now. It's different this time," he insisted.

"You've been saying that for twenty years. It isn't any different this time. It's the same as always." Joey stopped pacing, his face filled with hurt. "You promised me you stopped looking for the riddle. You lied to me!"

"No, son, I didn't lie to you."

Joey couldn't believe his ears. "I don't want anything to do with that map, that treasure, or you, ever again." Joey stormed out of the room and pushed past the crew.

"Wait," yelled the captain.

Joey stomped up the stairs, not waiting to hear the explanation.

"Joey, I found the riddle!"

Joey stopped in his tracks.

The crew gasped in excitement.

Joey walked slowly back into the room. "What did you say?"

"I be saying I found the riddle. After all these years. I would never lie to you, son. I did stop looking for the riddle, just like I said. I didn't need to look for it anymore, because I found it." Captain Dailey had a twinkle in his eye.

Joey stood there speechless. "Really?" he finally asked, his voice full of skepticism.

"Really. A couple months ago I be finding the riddle on a remote island. It was inscribed inside a hidden cave. Looking back, it shouldn't have taken me so long to find. The clues be obvious now that I figured out what they be saying. Now I just need to figure out the riddle in order to find the map."

Joey shook his head. "And that's just it. More clues, which will lead to more clues, which will lead to a treasure that doesn't exist."

"But the riddle exists!" The captain reached into a drawer and pulled out a small treasure chest. He took the ornate key from around his neck and unlocked it. He held up a dirty fragile piece of parchment. "It be right here."

Joey looked at the paper. His imagination was filled with images of buried treasure and endless stacks of gold coins. The excitement built up inside him. He felt like a kid again. Then he paused. "You know, that piece of parchment actually excited me. Just like you got me excited all those years ago when I was a kid." He pursed his lips. "And that excitement led to nothing but disappointment, and to a father who wasn't there." He shook his head. "I'm not going down that road again." He turned to walk out of the room.

"At least listen to the riddle before you go."

"No, I'm done. I'm happy for you that you found the riddle. But I'm not going to watch you waste your life away again, spending twenty more years searching for a map and then a treasure that you'll never find." Joey walked up the stairs.

The captain opened the piece of paper and spoke in a booming voice.

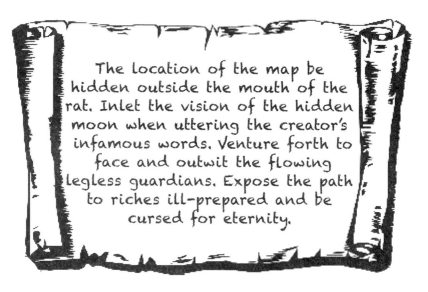

The location of the map be hidden outside the mouth of the rat. Inlet the vision of the hidden moon when uttering the creator's infamous words. Venture forth to face and outwit the flowing legless guardians. Expose the path to riches ill-prepared and be cursed for eternity.

Rusty grabbed a piece of parchment and wrote down the riddle furiously. He loved jokes and riddles and would be sure to enjoy it later.

Seconds passed without any noise. Then they heard Joey's footsteps coming down the stairs. He walked into the room. He and the captain looked at each other in silence.

Joey broke the silence. "I think I know where your treasure is."

The captain's eyes widened. "Aye?"

"Aye. The mouth of the rat. I was just there for an investment conference."

"Where?" asked Owen, his eyes filled with greed.

He ignored Owen and said to the captain, "Boca Raton, which means 'mouth of the rat' in Spanish."

"Boca Raton," the captain repeated. He looked off in the distance, searching his memory. "Aye, Blackbeard is said to have buried treasure there."

"I'm not sure what the rest of the riddle means, but I would head there," Joey said. "Good luck." He turned to walk away again.

"Come with us," said the captain. "It will just take a day. I could use your help."

Joey stopped and considered it. "No, I don't want to get involved."

"Think of the treasure, Giuseppe. Don't it be worth taking a day to see if it be true?"

The captain had a good point. From a risk-adjusted, time-weighted, mathematical point of view, it made a lot of sense. He could earn a huge return on investment without putting up any money, and by only taking one day of his time. The probability of finding something was now much higher since, unlike before, they had the riddle and a destination. His co-workers back in New York could cover his work. Plus, he could also use a little adventure.

Joey bit his lip. "Because my Wall Street buddies would say that this is a good trade, I will go. But only under one condition."

"Name it," said the captain.

"You stop calling me Giuseppe."

The captain smiled. "That's a deal, Joey." They shook hands, and then he pulled in Joey for a hug.

"It'll be good to have you aboard again," said the captain. "Crew, get ready to sail to Boca Raton. I'll put a list of supplies together that we'll need." The captain walked to the storage room to investigate what they would need for the trip.

"That be pretty impressive you figured out the riddle," Sandy told Joey.

"Well, I only figured out part of it. And let's see if my hunch is right."

"It still be impressive," she said with a slight smile.

Joey's heart leapt at the thought that she might be thawing toward him.

"Alright, here be the supplies we need." The captain brought over the list. "Who wants to get them?"

"I'm not sure where to go, but I can help," offered Joey.

"I'll help you," replied Sandy. "I can point you in the right direction to make sure you don't get lost."

"Well, thank you, Sandy," he said, smiling.

"You be welcome," said Sandy, returning his smile.

They held each other's gaze for only a few seconds, which was long enough for Joey to feel a warm feeling inside.

"I be going too, that be fun!" shouted Rusty, clearly oblivious to what was going on.

Sandy turned away, hoping to hide her blushing cheeks.

"That's terrific, Rusty," said Joey, trying not to grit his teeth. "Why don't you come join us?"

"Aye, aye!" Rusty had a big smile on his face.

"You all get the supplies," said the captain. "Owen and me be preparing the ship."

They said goodbye and parted ways.

"Sweet Calypso!" exclaimed Rusty as they walked away from the dock.

"What?" asked Joey, looking around.

"It be them." Rusty felt a nervous excitement.

Joey looked ahead and saw two girls walking toward them. Their straight blonde hair fell to just above their chests. In their early twenties, they carried themselves like nothing could hurt them. Their never-ending curves were accentuated by their tight-fitting clothing. One was dressed in white, the other in black.

"Ahoy, Rusty," said one of the girls.

"Ahoy, Tal," said Rusty, trying not to pant.

Joey saw that they were even more stunning up close. Then he almost fell over when he realized they were twins.

"What be going on?" asked Tal. "I just got back from talking to Don, and you'll never guess what he said." She noticed Rusty wasn't alone. "Who be your friends? Are they crewmates of yours? I be thinking I should work for Captain Dailey. I mean, he be so great and all. Anyway, I just be speaking to Don Harr and he said I should become a cook. Maybe I should be doing that? Did you know Don be dating Dawn Hardey now? Can you imagine, if they got married

60

it'd be the Hardey-Harr wedding. Wouldn't that be funny?"

"Aye," said Rusty. He couldn't decide which question to answer first. "This be Joey, and this be Sandy. Joey and Sandy, meet Tal Kalot."

"Nice to meet you," said Joey as he shook Tal's hand. Joey noticed her sister looking him up and down.

"Aye, nice to meet ya," said Sandy.

The other girl stepped forward. "Hi, I be her sister. Me name be Alicia, but I go by Lic." She looked Joey in the eyes and stuck out her hand, ignoring Sandy. "Nice to meet you, Joey." They shook hands, and she held onto his a little longer than expected. She subtly licked her lips.

Joey's heart started beating faster.

"What you be up to?" asked Tal. "We just went to get food and the cook told me his life story. Do you know his wife cheated on him last week? Oops, he said I wasn't supposed to say anything." She giggled. "Never mind, forget you heard that. Where you guys be going?"

"We be heading to get supplies," said Rusty. "We figured out Duarte's riddle and need to stock the ship!" He waved his note with the riddle on it.

Upon hearing this, Joey slapped his hand on his forehead.

Sandy stared at Rusty in disbelief.

"Really?" asked Tal excitedly.

"Haha, no that's not what he meant," laughed Joey. "He meant we are heading to find Duarte's riddle, which we think could be in a far off island. It's a wild goose chase, really. But we should get going, nice to meet you." He started to drag Rusty away while Rusty was asking what he did wrong.

"Wait, don't go yet," said Lic. She winked at him.

Joey stopped. He looked the twins up and down. He felt hypnotized by their Coke-bottle figures. "I guess we could stick around for a little bit longer."

Sandy slapped him on the arm. "No we can't! Need to be goin'. Bye." She dragged Joey away.

When they were out of earshot, Sandy said to Rusty, "Are you

61

crazy? Don't be telling anyone about the riddle!"

"Sorry, I didn't be realizing. I just be wanting to impress them."

Sandy tried to calm down. "How do you know them?"

"Tal be knowing everybody. She talks a lot, you can't keep her quiet."

"Argh," said Sandy. She pictured half the town knowing about their plan before they even got back to the ship.

CHAPTER ELEVEN

They walked to the store in silence. Eventually Sandy asked, "What did you be wanting to tell me before you stormed down to see the captain?"

"Huh?" asked Joey.

"You were going to respond to me taxes comment."

Joey tried to think back to their chat on the deck of the ship. So much had happened since then. "Oh right. I was saying how there is a way to avoid taxes for decades. Then you called me stupid for thinking that."

Sandy smirked.

"Well, guess what?" he continued. "It is possible. In fact, the government encourages it. They are called IRAs and 401(k)s."

Sandy didn't like being wrong, and it surprised her that it was possible to avoid taxes legally. "Did you think I be saying stupid?" She pondered for a moment. "I said stupendous." She smiled.

"Right..." he responded.

"I've been wantin' to learn about IRAs and 401(k)s," she said. "I just don't have any money at the end of the month to save for retirement."

"Guess what. Few people do, even if they make over a hundred thousand dollars a year."

This comment surprised Sandy. "How can people making that much not have any money left over? That don't be making sense."

Joey knew plenty of people who had high incomes but little wealth; they confused having a big paycheck with being rich.

"Somehow our expenses expand to however much money is available. Money has a way of slowly disappearing if we don't immediately set it aside. That is why the concept of Pay Yourself First is so important." He paused to let this concept sink in. "Most people pay the government first, then the rent or mortgage, then the electric company and the rest of the bills. They pay everyone else first and pay themselves last."

"But often times paying yourself first don't be possible," she objected.

"Everyone can do it if they put their minds to it."

"Really?"

"Yes. Robert Kiyosaki is a famous author who has helpful and unconventional perspectives on money and building wealth. He often tells a story about how his Rich Dad thinks about savings. Every month, his Rich Dad would put aside money for his investments. He did this no matter what, even if he didn't have enough to cover his other expenses. Paying himself first motivated him to work harder because he had bills to pay."

Sandy asked, "But what if he ran out of money by the end of the month and couldn't pay a bill?"

"He never missed a payment. He used the fear of not being able to pay his bills to motivate him to make more money."

"How did he be making more money?"

"He worked extra jobs, started companies, traded in the stock market – anything he could to make sure he met his obligations. He said, 'If I had paid myself last, I would have felt no pressure... but I'd also be broke.' The bottom line is that you need to pay yourself first, because if you don't, no one else will."

They arrived at the general store and went inside. There were products everywhere. It had all the supplies they would need for the trip. Two elderly pirates at the register greeted them.

Rusty looked around the store and spotted something that made him jump for joy. "Look, look!" he exclaimed. He ran over to a live parrot.

Joey and Sandy followed him.

"Look at him, he be perfect. I need him. Can I buy him? I'd

64

name him Petey." Rusty looked at Joey with hopeful eyes.

"Petey the Pirate Parrot, huh?" Joey pictured the parrot sitting on Rusty's shoulder. He could almost hear them talking to each other. Joey knew Rusty wasn't going to like his answer, but Rusty needed to learn he couldn't always have what he wanted. "I look at things in terms of wants and needs. Do you need this parrot or want this parrot?"

"Every real pirate needs a parrot, matey."

"I'm not asking about pirates in general. I'm asking about you specifically. Do you need this parrot, or do you want this parrot?"

Rusty lowered his head. "I guess I only be wanting it."

"I think you're right."

Rusty looked like he wanted to start pouting.

"But buying things you want isn't always a bad thing," continued Joey. "Part of the joy of being financially secure is that you can blow your money on silly things you don't need."

"Really? So I can buy it?" Rusty became excited again.

"It depends. You need to be able to comfortably afford your wants. I live by the Ten Times Test."

"What be that?" asked Sandy.

"The Ten Times Test says that when it comes to something you want, you should have at least ten times that amount in savings. If you don't, that means you are spending over 10% of your life savings on something you don't even need." He turned to Rusty. "How much does the parrot cost?"

Rusty looked at the price tag. "It be costing five-hundred doubloons."

"Do you have ten times that amount, meaning five-thousand doubloons, in savings?"

"Not even close!" Rusty became pouty again. "But I be having twenty-seven doubloons of savings."

Joey pursed his lips. "Yeah, I think it's better if you don't spend your money on the parrot. Do you agree?"

Rusty pretended like he didn't hear him.

"Rusty?" Joey said.

"Aye, you be right," Rusty said as he crossed his arms and looked away.

"Listen, I'm not saying you can never buy the parrot. I want you to buy luxury items and I want you to enjoy having them, I really do. I just want you to be able to comfortably afford them first." Joey paused. "Think delay. You're not saying no to yourself forever. You are just delaying the purchase until later. In fact, if you wait to buy something, you might realize that you didn't really want it in the first place. Think delay."

Knowing that he could get the parrot later made Rusty feel better. "Aye, I should save more doubloons before I go making a big purchase like that."

"Aye," Sandy said in a sad voice. Joey saw her staring at a beautiful opal necklace. Within the stone, an array of colors bounced off each other in its milky white chamber, enchanting the eye as it glistened. The fiery reds, ice-cold blues, burning yellows, soft greens, and warming pinks all sparkled together as it drew her deeper into its mystery.

"Quite a magical stone, isn't it?" asked Joey.

"It's so beautiful. Look at the colors." She turned to look at him. "What is it?"

"It's an opal, my favorite gemstone," he said.

"Really?"

"Yes. The opal is a mysterious stone with a rich and varied folklore."

"Tell me," she said, wide-eyed.

"It is said to get its name from Ops, the Roman goddess of fertility. In ancient Rome, the opal was valued above all other gems. Caesars regularly gave the dazzling multi-colored stone to their wives. It was called the 'Cupid Stone,' and it's said to have sparked the romance between Mark Antony and Cleopatra."

"How romantic," she said.

"In the Middle Ages, the opal was a source of great luck. They said it possessed the virtues of all the other gemstones whose colors it contained. It was said to have the mystical powers of curing all eye ailments, and when wrapped in a bay leaf, would give the owner the power of invisibility."

"Fascinating." Her eyes sparkled with each additional detail.

"Then in the 1800s, Sir Walter Scott wrote about the opal in one of his novels. He did it in a way that gave the stone a reputation for bringing bad luck and even death. This caused the opal to be unloved for fifty years."

"How sad." She frowned at the thought.

"But then the majestic black opal was discovered in Australia. This skyrocketed its popularity, and it has been well-loved ever since. Today the seductive stone is associated with intensifying the states of love and passion, and due to its absorbent and reflective nature, is said to increase creativity."

She felt breathless after hearing the story. "How you be knowing this?"

"I know a lot of things." He winked at her.

She smiled and turned away. Then she looked at the necklace again. "Too bad I can't be affording this. It be beautiful."

"You have the wrong mindset," Joey corrected her. "That's how ordinary people think, not how the wealthy think."

"What do you mean?"

"Average people say to themselves, 'I can't afford this'. People driven to succeed ask themselves, 'How can I afford this?' The subconscious mind is a powerful tool, and how you talk to yourself can influence your destiny."

"Really?" she asked, her face full of skepticism.

"Successful people truly believe they can become rich. They feed their mind with encouraging language to help them accomplish their goals. All successful people have hit multiple roadblocks; at any point they could have given up. But they didn't. They believed in their destiny to achieve success, and they told their mind to keep moving forward."

Rusty bit his lip and shook his head. "That sounds like that positive thinking stuff I be hearing about. That just be rainbows and angelfish kind of talk."

"It's not so much positive thinking as it is having an unwavering

67

confidence in yourself. Let me ask you a question. Are you rich?" asked Joey.

"Huh?" asked Rusty.

"I said, are you rich?"

"No," Rusty said, frowning.

"Go ask a rich person if they think what I said is a bunch of rainbows and angelfish talk. I bet they'll agree with it completely."

Rusty pondered his comment. "It be a nice thought," he admitted. "And I'm sure it will help a little. But I can't ever become really rich."

"You know what Henry Ford would say to that?" asked Joey.

"Who's Henry Ford?"

"He was one of the greatest businessmen of the twentieth century. He had a great quote which said, 'Whether you think you can, or you think you can't – you're right.'"

Sandy looked back at the necklace. "So you be saying if I ask meself how can I afford this necklace, my mind will give me the answer?"

"That's right. I'm not an expert on this stuff like Tony Robbins, but it works. It may not be an easy answer, and you may not get an answer right away. But if you focus enough on something and do what it takes, you will eventually get the answer to whatever question you ask yourself."

Sandy was skeptical, but figured there was no harm in trying it. She thought of many areas in her life where she wanted to try this method.

CHAPTER TWELVE

Sandy, Joey, and Rusty continued their shopping. Near the front of the store Joey saw something that excited him: a stunning globe. Its hand-carved wooden base had ornamental carvings along the bottom. A golden axis held the globe in place while he spun it. He ran his fingers along its surface, feeling the various topographies around the world. Since Joey had not traveled much internationally, this stimulated his imagination as to all the world had to offer.

Sandy joined him. Together, they spun the globe over and over again, looking at the vast array of countries and terrain. She stopped the globe and pointed to a specific spot. "That's where I be wanting to go." She was pointing to Huahine in French Polynesia, an island in the South Pacific. "I hear it be beautiful there. I want to lie on its untouched sandy beaches, smell its vanilla plantations, feed the large eels with their translucent blue eyes, and explore its ancient temples."

"Sounds amazing," said Joey.

"There be so many places to explore." She spun the globe a few more times. "This globe is beautiful."

"Yes, I have always wanted a globe like this," he said.

"Aye, well it be your lucky day then."

"Yes it is," Joey said as he looked into her eyes and felt at peace with himself.

"I think she be talking about the globe, matey," said Rusty.

"Of course, so was I," said Joey, feeling a sudden warmth in his cheeks. He started to walk toward the checkout.

"Wait," said Sandy.

He turned around, eager to hear what she had to say.

"Aren't you going to buy it?"

"Buy what?"

"This globe that you be wanting for so long?"

Joey looked at the globe and saw the price tag said four-hundred doubloons. "For four-hundred doubloons? Ha. This is definitely a want, not a need. Sure, it would bring me a lot of enjoyment. And even though it passes the Ten Times Test for me, do you know how much four-hundred doubloons will be worth thirty years from now with the power of compound interest?"

Sandy scoffed and walked away. She couldn't see herself with someone who was such a penny pincher and who was so cheap all the time.

"He be making a good point, you know," said the older pirate behind the counter. "That be an important lesson all young people should be knowing."

Sandy asked, "Why do you say that?"

The shorter man wore a Hawaiian shirt with a straw hat. The taller man wore a polo shirt with the name of the general store embroidered on it.

"Take me and me brother here. Me brother be Bill Foldes."

"Nice to meet ya," said Bill as he tipped his hat.

"Hi, I'm Joey."

"I be seventy-one years young and Bill be seventy. Me brother started saving for retirement when he be twenty-five. He saved three-hundred doubloons per month for fifteen years. Then at forty he got divorced and stopped saving. He ain't saved a penny since."

Bill nodded, indicating that it was true.

"Me, on the other hand, when I was twenty-five I be focused on partying and blowing me money on whatever I wanted."

"That be the way!" said Rusty.

"The thought never crossed me mind to save, since no one told me I should. If I'd known better, I'd have started earlier. But what can you do? I finally started saving at forty years of age. I've been saving three-hundred doubloons a month for the past thirty years.

Me brother and I have been earning about 8% each year on our money. So whatcha think? Which of us has more money today?"

"That be easy," said Sandy. "You've been saving for twice as long as your brother Bill, and Bill hasn't saved any money in 30 years. You be having more money."

"I agree," said Rusty.

Joey remained silent.

"Let's find out," the man said. "I have 450,000 doubloons today. Bill, how much do you have?"

Bill answered, "I be having a little over one million doubloons."

"Really?" said Sandy. She turned to Joey. "Is that possible?"

"Of course it is," said Joey. "That is the magic of compound interest and the power of starting early."

"Now I be working for me brother Bill," he continued. "He owns this shop and I still have to work. I wish I be startin' early like him."

"You started saving at age twenty-five," Sandy said. "I be twenty-three, so I don't need to start saving for two more years then?"

"No, the earlier the better," said Joey. "Say you started investing fifty doubloons a month when you were thirteen years old. Today at twenty-three you could already have close to 10,000 doubloons. And by the time you turn seventy-five that money could grow into over half a million doubloons, even if you didn't add another penny from this day forward."

"Shiver me timbers!" she said. "I'm gonna tell me thirteen-year-old niece that. When she be older and has all that extra treasure, she can buy me a whale skin coat."

Joey's nose wrinkled at her remark. "Whale skin?" He shrugged his shoulders. "Whatever floats your boat, or pirate ship. But yeah, tell her to start saving now."

Sandy looked in her basket and put a couple items back on the shelf.

The older brother rang up the few items Joey needed for the trip. Joey handed him a credit card.

"What you be doing?" shouted Rusty.

"What?" asked Joey.

"You be scolding me for using me credit cards, and you be using one yourself. You said you be hating credit cards."

"I never said I hated credit cards. I said I hated credit card debt. How can you expect to get ahead when you're paying twenty percent interest to the credit cards companies? But credit cards aren't evil; they actually have several benefits. The difference is that I have a zero balance on my credit cards, and I pay it off every month."

"Ah."

They finished ringing up all the items, including food, drinks, gunpowder, and matches. Rusty purchased several bags of Chips Ahoy cookies, which he claimed was the only dessert for a true pirate. They said good-bye to the brothers and left the store.

⚔ ⚔ ⚔

They walked back toward the ship, supplies in hand. Rusty wanted to walk briskly to get back to the ship, which left Joey and Sandy alone to talk.

"That be amazing Bill be a millionaire. You wouldn't have guessed by lookin' at him," said Sandy.

"A lot of wealthy people don't look rich, and they probably like it that way."

"I wonder if he be single," she laughed.

"Gee, what a surprise. A pirate who's a gold digger," laughed Joey.

"I just be joking."

"I know. Besides, no other guy would be as good as me, anyway."

"Well, no other girl you find would be as good as me," she said back.

Joey decided not to comment on how unoriginal her response was. Instead, he asked, "Oh yeah, what makes you so special?"

She thought about his question. "I take care of meself; I be a hard worker. I'm gonna make a great mom, and I'll take great care of me man if he be worthy."

Joey nodded, impressed. "Those actually are good qualities." He added with a smile, "Too bad you're kind of a dork."

"Ha, whatever. You know you'd want to be the man I'd be taking great care of." She quickly changed the topic before he had a chance to deny this. "But back to the brothers, should that be me goal?

One million doubloons for retirement?"

Joey took in a deep breath. "That is a big question today. Everyone wants to know, what is their number for retirement? Is it half a million, a million, four million, twenty million? The answer is that it depends on your needs and goals. You can use online retirement calculators to help you figure out a personalized number."

"What be an online retirement calculator?" she asked.

"I guess pirate ships don't come with computers. Well, Fidelity is a large financial company that has a specialty in retirement planning. They came out with a general rule of thumb for figuring out the minimum amount you'll need. By the time you retire at age sixty-seven, you should have at least eight times your final salary saved."

"How much be that for me?" asked Sandy.

"It assumes you plan to retire at sixty-seven years old. How much do you think you'll be making at sixty-seven?"

"75,000 doubloons a year."

"Alright. Eight times 75,000 is 600,000 doubloons, so you should have at least that much saved before retirement."

Sandy didn't feel that optimistic anymore about her retirement. "That be a lot of treasure."

"Yes, but you don't have to save it all at once. You should be accumulating it over time."

"How much should I be having already?"

Joey explained Fidelity's guidelines to Sandy.

AGE	AMOUNT SAVED OF SALARY
30	50%
35	1x
45	3x
55	5x
67	8x

"The first milestone they have is at age 30. How much do you plan to make when you're thirty years old?"

"50,000 doubloons per year."

"According to this chart, by the time you are thirty you should already have 25,000 doubloons saved for retirement, which is 50% of 50,000."

Sandy realized she may need to make more money. "What if I be wanting to make 100,000 doubloons at age thirty-five and 200,000 doubloons at age sixty-seven?"

Joey calculated the numbers in his head. "Then you should have 100,000 doubloons saved by age thirty-five and 1,600,000 doubloons by age sixty-seven."

Sandy gulped at hearing these even higher numbers.

"Remember, this is just a rule of thumb. It makes a lot of assumptions that may or may not be true for everyone."

"Like what?"

"It assumes you start saving 6% to your 401(k) at age twenty-five, and you steadily raise your contribution to 12% by your early thirties. It assumes you'll retire at sixty-seven, and you will get social security. Using these guidelines, you should be able to replace 85% of your ending salary."

"Wouldn't I need to replace 100% of my salary?" asked Sandy.

"In general, most people spend less money in retirement than during their working years." Joey thought of the typical grandparents who had the house paid off, kids living on their own, and were living a comfortable life without too much excitement. They usually spent more on medical expenses but less on everything else. "You may need to save more or less than 600,000 doubloons. Personally I think 600,000 doubloons by retirement is too low. ING is another financial company, and they have the ING Your Number website. It says you would need over 3,000,000 doubloons by retirement to achieve similar results. The math all depends on the assumptions you use and what your specific circumstances are. Just know that it is better to start saving now rather than later."

"That be a lot of treasure." She let out a sigh. "I better start saving, and keep saving for a long time. But what if I be having questions? Can you walk me through everything?"

Joey stepped back and held up his hands up in an overly dramatic fashion. "Whoa, slow down there, girl," he said with a smile. "We just met and you're already asking me to see you all the time and 'help you with your homework?' We should slow things down a little."

Sandy's jaw dropped in surprise upon hearing his comment, but her eyes were smiling. She started to laugh. "I be serious though, that be a lot of money to save by thirty."

"25,000 doubloons absolutely is a lot of money. But if you want to become wealthy, then 25,000 isn't that much when compared to being a millionaire. You need to reframe your mind and raise the expectations you set for yourself."

Sandy thought about this. She wondered if she wasn't setting high enough goals for herself. She decided to change that right away. "Aye. 25,000 doubloons be nothing. I'm gonna be a millionaire by thirty!" she exclaimed, only halfway believing it.

"There you go, that's a better way to think. But you can't just think it. You need to put a plan in place."

"Aye." She had no idea how to make a million doubloons, but felt she better start figuring it out.

CHAPTER THIRTEEN

Rusty came running back to Joey and Sandy. He looked scared. "What's wrong?" asked Sandy.

Panting, he pointed behind him. Joey saw two pirates with purple bandanas running toward them. Their pistols were drawn. It was Ivan and Macon.

Joey didn't know why they were being chased or what their intentions were, and he didn't want to find out. "Run!" he shouted.

They dropped their supplies and ran as fast as they could. Their pursuers broke into an all-out sprint. Joey, Rusty, and Sandy saw a shop ahead and darted inside, avoiding the customers as they rushed past them. In the back of the store they saw an exit door, which they ran to and burst through it. Joey glanced back and saw Ivan and Macon gaining on them. Rushing through the door, they found themselves in a large sculpture garden surrounded by a tall fence. They were trapped.

"Crap!" shouted Joey. He stuck his head back in the store and saw their pursuers making their way toward them. Ivan and Macon were pushing customers out of the way, knocking merchandise off the shelves. Joey pulled his head back outside, slamming the door shut. Out of the corner of his eye he saw a wooden board; he ran to grab it and anchored it under the handle. "This way!" he commanded. They ran to the back corner of the garden next to a large pile of rocks and hid behind a sculpture of Minerva.

They heard banging on the door as Ivan tried to dislodge the wooden board. After a few seconds of pounding, gun shots rang through the air and the door squealed open. Joey looked around for an escape. Their only option was to climb the fence, but it was impossible to do that unnoticed. He snuck a glance and saw Ivan and Macon in the opposite corner, pistols drawn, moving slowly through the sculptures as if expecting to be ambushed. Joey didn't dare move and tried to be as silent as possible. He even slowed his breath out of fear they may hear his panting.

Out of the silence came the crash of rocks falling. He turned and saw Rusty standing there holding a rock with a shocked look on his face. Joey couldn't believe it. He then turned and accidently made eye contact with Ivan, who immediately started running toward them.

"Climb the fence!" Joey shouted. Rusty and Sandy climbed as fast as they could while Joey threw two rocks over the fence. Ivan maneuvered through the sculptures quickly but Macon tripped over one and fell. Joey was halfway up the fence when he felt a hand grab his foot; he looked down and saw Ivan trying to pull him down. Joey kicked furiously and was able to knock off his boot, causing Ivan to fall back. Ivan threw the boot and started climbing. As soon as Joey hit the ground on the other side, he rushed over to the first rock and chucked it at Ivan. It missed, so he picked up the second rock and threw it directly at Ivan's head. The impact knocked him back and disoriented him for a few precious seconds.

"Let's go!" shouted Sandy as she ran ahead of him. Joey took off his other boot and ran to catch up. He looked out over the landscape ahead. It was wide-open space until the shoreline, where there was a collection of palm trees and boulders. "Head that way!" he shouted as he took a quick look back. Ivan was already over the fence in pursuit, and Macon was almost to the other side.

Rusty was a surprisingly fast runner, but he could see Sandy was getting tired. If they could make it to the shoreline then the ship shouldn't be too far off and they could yell for help. They continued running, and Joey sensed Ivan was gaining quickly.

Almost to the shoreline, he heard Sandy scream. He turned and saw that Ivan had grabbed her arm and was pulling her toward him. Joey turned on a dime and ran straight for Ivan. Ivan didn't see him coming, and Joey kicked him right between the legs. Ivan collapsed to the ground, and Joey and Sandy ran away with all their might.

"I think we might make it!" shouted Joey, feeling a rush of excitement. What he heard next sent ice-cold water through his veins. Gunshots. They dove behind the nearest boulder.

Joey knew they didn't have a chance unless they retaliated. "Rusty, do you have any pistols?"

"Pistols? Why would I be carrying pistols to go shopping?"

"I do," said Sandy as she reached down and pulled out two pistols, handing one to Joey.

"That a girl," Joey said with a smile. He examined the gun, turning it around in his hand. He wasn't sure if it was ready to fire or if he had to do something.

Sandy leaned over and cocked his pistol.

"Thanks," Joey said sheepishly. They both popped up above the boulder and returned fire. They caught their pursuers completely off guard, forcing them to dive behind a nearby boulder. Joey fired a couple more shots at their adversaries' position, but his bullets weren't following his aim.

"You're shot be way off," said Sandy. "Aim directly at them."

"I'm trying," Joey said in frustration. He sat back down behind the boulder. "This is crazy." He figured there must be a way to reason with them. "What do you guys want?" he shouted.

"We know you have the riddle, and Captain Goodman wants it," shouted back Ivan. "Hand it over now, or we'll pry it from your cold dead hands!"

They all knew how dangerous it would be if Captain Goodman got possession of Duarte's treasure. They had to prevent that at all costs.

"We can't give it to them," said Rusty, a look of fear in his eyes.

"I know." Joey noticed the captain's ship in the distance and he became hopeful. They could try to make a run for it, but he knew it was too dangerous. "Rusty," he said sternly, "I need you to run to the ship and get help. We'll give you cover. Run as fast as you can."

"Aye aye!" Before Joey had a chance to say go, Rusty started running. Joey and Sandy popped out to the side of the boulder and fired both guns with full force at Ivan and Macon.

Cowering behind their boulder, Ivan and Macon returned fire. They stuck their firing hands out to the side, not daring to raise their heads with the shower of bullets raining down upon them.

Sandy ran out of bullets and ducked down to reload. Joey continued firing. Even though he aimed directly at them, the bullets weren't following his path. Ivan peeked his head out and Joey fired at him, but his bullet ricocheted off a neighboring boulder. Ivan smiled and popped out above the boulder for a split second. He fired at Joey, hitting him squarely in the shoulder. Joey dropped for cover, pressing his body up against the boulder as his shoulder throbbed with intense pain.

"You've been shot!" shouted Sandy, as she saw him bleeding though his shirt. She grabbed his pistol. Filled with rage, she fired continuously at their enemies, causing Ivan to duck for cover again. She didn't stop shooting. Pieces of boulder flew off in all directions, the continuous bang of the shots echoing through the air. She fired shot after shot in anger until she was empty. She looked at the pistol, filled with fear. "We be out of bullets," she said to Joey.

"What's that I hear?" said Ivan. "You be out of bullets? That's funny, because we be having plenty. See?"

Joey and Sandy heard five bullets smash into their boulder.

"It looks like this game be over," shouted Ivan. "Hand over the riddle! Or face the consequences."

Joey peeked out and saw Ivan and Macon walking toward them with big smiles, knowing they'd scored another victory. How could he have allowed himself to get into this situation? He knew he should have left when he had the chance; Duarte's map brought nothing but trouble. Joey looked around, but couldn't see any escape. He said a prayer in silence as he prepared for the inevitable.

Ivan was halfway to their location when they suddenly heard a blast. Then they felt an explosion rock them backward. Joey and Sandy looked around. "What was that?" he asked.

They saw and heard three more explosions right in front of them. Joey noticed the Captain's ship cruising forward.

"They're firing the cannons at us!" shouted Ivan. "Run!"

Ivan and Macon ran as they heard eleven more blasts coming from the ocean. Seconds later, an explosive rain of fire, shrapnel, dirt, and boulder came down around them. The once-peaceful field was now a fireball of destruction. Six more blasts came from the ship, causing them to run even faster.

Sandy rejoiced seeing them run for dear life. But her joy turned to fear when she looked at Joey. He was pale and losing consciousness. She gave Joey a hug, but he grunted in pain upon the embrace. She cradled him in her arms, hoping help would arrive before it was too late.

CHAPTER FOURTEEN

The captain, Rusty, and Owen ran over to Joey, who was lying behind the boulder.

"This be unbelievable! I feel horrible," said the captain. "How ye be?"

"It's a bit painful, but I think I'll be fine," said Joey.

"We be taking you to the doctor right away. I know a specialist for this kind of injury. We be heading there right now."

They waited in the lobby of the doctor's office. After a few minutes, the doctor came out. He was a tall black man with a solid build, and appeared to be in his forties. He wore a traditional white coat but Joey was surprised to see he wore an eye patch. The doctor smiled at them warmly.

"Ahoy. I be Dr. Aiken."

The captain stood up to shake the doctor's hand. "Pleased to meet you, doctor. I be hearing good things about you. This here be me son. I be wanting you to take the best care of him. Treasure be of no concern, I be paying whatever it costs. Give him the best treatment, aye?"

"Aye aye, Captain, and it be a pleasure to meet ya. You be an inspiration to the pirate community, and it be an honor to know ye."

"Me be appreciating your kind words."

Dr. Aiken took Joey back to medical room.

Joey sat on the table and looked at the pictures and degrees on the wall. "You don't strike me as a pirate."

Dr. Aiken examined the wound. "Oh, that's because I'm not. However, I've found if I talk like one it makes the patients feel more comfortable."

"Is that why you wear the eye patch?"

He shook his head. "Oh no, the eye patch is real. I had a fishing accident when I was younger."

Dr. Aiken began treating the wound. The sanitizing liquid stung, causing Joey to cringe. He gritted his teeth but tried to not let the pain get to him. "Is that what made you become a doctor?"

"No, I always knew I wanted to be a doctor. But the accident helped me figure out what niche I wanted to be in. In today's business world, you can't be all things to all people. You really need to pick a niche and specialize in it. I figured since I wore an eye patch I might as well specialize in pirates."

"How's that worked out?"

The doctor grabbed a clean bandage. "It's been great. Turns out pirates get hurt a lot, so my practice has been booming. Once a pirate discovers I specialize in their specific needs, they send all their friends to me. They even send their enemies! Pirates sail in from around the world to get my treatment." He put the final piece of tape on the bandage. "Alright, you're all set."

"That's it? Am I going to be okay?"

"You'll be fine. It was just a flesh wound, and the bullet went straight through. You should be completely healed in a couple weeks."

"Great. Thank you, doctor."

"Anytime," he replied.

Joey returned to the waiting room.

"How was it?" the captain and Sandy asked at the same time.

"He said I'll make a full recovery."

"Aye, that be great to hear," said the captain. He looked relieved.

Joey sat down to tell them what the doctor said. After a couple of minutes, the door flung open and a woman came running in from outside.

It was Lic.

She rushed over to Joey. "I just heard what be happening," she said, sitting in the empty seat next to him. "How you be feeling?"

"What you be doing here?" snarled Sandy. "You told the whole town about the riddle. We wouldn't even be here if it wasn't for you."

"No," Lic exclaimed. "It wasn't me, it was my sister. I promise. I told her not to say anything, but she never listens. I be feelin' so bad." She put her hand on his knee.

"That's okay, I believe you." Joey enjoyed her attention and felt drawn to her physical beauty. He couldn't stop admiring her body, but was torn between his feelings for her and Sandy. He could see the potential for a deeper connection developing with Sandy, whereas his attraction to Lic seemed more superficial.

Lic looked in his eyes and pressed up against him. "I'm really sorry. My sister has such a big mouth. But they shouldn't have done this to you. Those bad, bad men." She ran her fingers through his hair. "Don't worry, I'll take care of you from now on."

"Oh no, you won't," said Sandy. She stood up and crossed her arms, giving Lic a stare that would scare sharks away.

Lic returned her stare and smiled. "Of course I will." She hopped out of her seat and grabbed two lollipops from the jar on the counter. She sat down next to Joey. "I know what be making you feel better." She unwrapped one of the lollipops, put it in her mouth, and wrapped her tongue around it. Then she handed him the other lollipop.

Mesmerized by her skill with the lollipop, Joey replied, "Thank you."

"That be enough," said Sandy to Lic. "We can take care of him from here. You can be going now."

"Let's see what Joey here has to say. Do you want me to go?" Lic asked as she made a pouty face.

The captain and Rusty didn't move or say anything, not wanting to get involved. Owen walked off in frustration, not wanting to see anymore.

Joey looked at Lic, then at Sandy. He felt confused and not sure what to do. He had never had two beautiful women fighting over him before. It was something he had dreamed about, but now that it was happening it made him feel uncomfortable. He had a feeling he knew which one to pick, but he felt it was too early to make a decision.

"Listen, ladies, there is no need to cause a lot of drama here. I just got shot after all. Let's take it a day at a time and see what happens."

Lic and Sandy both gave him a disgusted look.

"No," said Lic. "Make a decision. You either pick me, or I'm gone."

He looked at her, looked at Sandy, then back at Lic. "I'm just not ready to make a decision yet," he said hesitantly.

"Arrgh." Lic threw her lollipop on the ground and stormed off. The door slammed behind her.

Joey sat down in his chair, feeling sad.

Sandy sat next to him. She played with his hair, looking at the door where Lic left. She smiled smugly.

The receptionist brought over the bill and handed it to Joey. Joey looked at it and was surprised by the high amount. "Good thing I have my emergency fund," he said to himself. Sandy looked at him with an intrigued look on her face as he reached into his pocket to pay.

"Hold on," said the captain. "You're not paying. I feel responsible for yer troubles." He handed the receptionist a handful of doubloons. "Here ya go."

"Wait, you don't have to do that," objected Joey. "I have money saved for this kind of thing."

"I don't care what you be having," said the captain. "I'm paying for it, and that's settled."

"Well, thank you. I appreciate that." Joey noticed Owen had wandered back in to join them.

"What be an emergency fund?" asked Sandy.

Joey and the others got up to leave the office. "It is also known as a rainy day fund. It is the first and most important step toward achieving financial freedom."

"We be pirates that sail the high seas, matey," said Rusty. "A rainy day fund be sounding like something for landlubbers. Can we call it a hurricane fund?"

"Sure, Rusty, let's call it a hurricane fund."

"Why we be needing one of those? I be just fine without it," said Owen.

"Maybe you've been fine so far, and if so, you're lucky. But unfortunately, an emergency eventually happens to all of us. It's important to have money ready for when it does. When most people have an emergency, they not only have the stress of the emergency, but also the stress of figuring out how to pay for it."

"That's what credit cards be for," said Owen.

"No, credit cards are not for emergencies. Your emergency fund, or rather your hurricane fund, is for emergencies. You don't want to have credit card debt, period. Don't use a credit card as an excuse to not do the prudent thing by building up a hurricane fund."

"How much money should be in it?" asked Sandy.

"It should be enough money to cover between three to eight months of expenses."

Rusty counted on his fingers. "That be a lot of treasure!"

"Yes it is. But it is very important that you do it, and many finance experts agree. For example, Dave Ramsey has an effective seven-step program to achieve financial freedom. His first step is to save $1000 in an emergency fund."

"Should I do that after I save for retirement?" asked Sandy.

"No, you should save $1000 right away. Do this even before paying down debt or saving for retirement."

"What be counting as an emergency?" asked Sandy.

"There is no definitive list, but the main reason to have it is in case you lose your job. You still need to pay your bills if you lose your job, and that's what the emergency fund is for. You can also use it for medical expenses, or if your car or house needs urgent repairs."

"Do going on a once-in-a-lifetime vacation for a *Pirates of the Caribbean* party count as an emergency?" asked Rusty.

"No, it doesn't," said Joey.

"But it be once in a lifetime. How can me pay for it?" Rusty asked.

"Figure out a different way to get the money. Work more hours, sell some stuff on eBay, start a small business as a babysitter or doing door-to-door sales. There are lots of ways to make money if you put your mind to it. But don't use your emergency fund for non-emergencies."

"Eight months of cash be a lot of treasure," said Sandy. "Should I invest it to make it grow even more?"

Joey shook his head. "No. The emergency fund should be in cash in a savings account and not used for anything else. The worst thing that can happen is you invest it, the stock market crashes, and you don't have enough money for the emergency."

They all nodded their heads in agreement. They walked back to the ship in silence as they digested the importance of having an emergency fund.

CHAPTER FIFTEEN

They returned to the ship and breathed a collective sigh of relief. "It's good to be back," said Rusty with a smile.

"Aye," said the captain.

Joey saw the supplies sitting in the corner. "You picked up the supplies that we dropped?"

"Aye. Rusty told me where they be, so I be having Owen get them."

"Thanks, Owen."

"Whatever," said Owen as he walked by to prepare the ship.

"Alright, crew," said the captain. "Let's go get us the lost treasure map of Duarte Bonaventura. Set sails for Boca Raton!"

The crew cheered in excitement.

They were well on their way to Boca and the sun was setting over the ocean. Joey admired the sunset and its beauty took his breath away. As they glided forward toward the ends of the earth, the sky was filled with deep purple atop silent pink atop indigo blue. The sounds of symphonic crashing waves filled his ears. A cascade of pinks, blues, and yellows rippled across the water. It was like nothing he had ever experienced.

Sandy came up beside him. "Isn't it beautiful?"

"It really is," Joey said softly. He continued looking at the sunset, his nostrils taking in Sandy's delicious scent; tonight she smelled of coconut and vanilla.

They stood there together watching the sun set until the ocean swallowed it whole, leaving behind a splattering of stars across the night sky.

After the evening performance, they attended to chores around the ship. They grabbed two buckets of soapy water and began scrubbing the deck.

As they scrubbed, Sandy said, "I've been meaning to ask you..."

"Yes?" asked Joey.

"You mentioned 401(k)s and IRAs before. What be those?"

Joey had hoped for a more exciting question, but took it in stride. "The 401(k) and IRA are a great way to save for retirement without having to pay taxes yet."

"And the governor won't be sending the militia on me for not paying the taxes?"

"You're so bad the governor is going to send the militia on you regardless." He smiled.

"Hardee har har." Sandy faked a laugh. She pushed Joey in a friendly way.

Owen saw them from across the ship, laughing and touching each other. Jealousy grew inside him.

Joey continued, "But yes, it is pre-tax money, so it's not subject to any taxes right now. It grows tax-deferred, so you don't have to pay taxes on any of the profits along the way. But you'll have to pay taxes on it when you eventually take out the money."

"And I can take out the money at any time if I need it?"

"No, definitely not. IRAs and 401(k)s are meant for retirement. If you take it out early you have to pay taxes and a penalty charge. You basically can't take it out until after you are fifty-nine and a half years old. You'll be old and wrinkly by then." He winked.

"Hey!" She smiled and splashed water on him from her bucket. "You be meaning to say I'll be a beautiful queen by then."

"A queen? Well then, you'll need a crown, your highness." He scooped bubbles from his bucket and plopped them in a circle on her head.

She gasped in surprise and delight.

"We'll see about you becoming a queen," said Joey. "I'll definitely be a king by then."

"A king, huh? Well, all true kings have a mustache so you better be gettin' one."

"No, they don't," he objected.

"Oh, yes they do. Look at the king in a deck of cards."

She did have a point, he thought. He then felt a bunch of bubbles on his mouth and heard her giggling.

"There be your mustache, your highness," she laughed.

"You got it all over my lips, not above my lips."

"Oh, you be right. Let me wipe them off for you." She moved her fingers close to him, and gently caressed the bubbles off his lips, letting her fingers linger. They locked eyes and without thinking, their lips moved toward each other like two celestial bodies drawn together by an invisible force.

"I want to play!" shouted Rusty, seeing the bubbles on their heads.

"Impeccable timing, as usual," growled Joey.

"What you be playing?" asked Rusty. "I like bubbles."

"We're playing who can be the quietest, and you're not winning," said Joey.

"Oh," said Rusty, frowning.

"Actually, Rusty," said Sandy, "we were playing learn about 401(k)s and IRAs. Want to listen in?"

"Aye," said Rusty, disappointed that the game didn't sound like more fun.

"Continue, your highness," Sandy said with a smile.

"Right then." He collected his thoughts. "You should set up your 401(k) or IRA for automatic deduction from your paycheck, then have the money be automatically invested. This is a great way to pay yourself first. You want it to all happen automatically so you don't have to think about it."

"Yarr," said Rusty. "That be sounding like a good plan for a lazy pirate."

"Exactly. Plus, with money automatically taken from your

paycheck, you never see it missing from your bank account. You hardly know the money is gone."

Sandy nodded as she continued scrubbing the deck. "What be the difference between an IRA and 401(k)?"

"An IRA is something you set up on your own, whereas you get access to a 401(k) through your employer. Many companies have a 401(k) program but not all of them do. Non-profits will often have 403(b) plans, which is similar to a 401(k). Some companies and organizations will even provide a match on your contributions where they give you free money. You'd have to be pretty dumb to not take this free money, but a lot of people leave it on the table."

"Aye," said Rusty. "Free treasure be hard to find. I be digging hundreds of holes looking for buried treasure and found nothing."

"For retirement it isn't the X that marks the spot. It's the K, as in 401(k). Contribute as much as you can. The money you contribute will always be yours, even if you leave the company. As for the money from the company match, you can keep that too, as long as you're fully vested."

"Vested? Like the vests ladies wear?" asked Rusty.

Owen overheard the chatter and came over to listen. However, he didn't grab a brush to help scrub.

"While girls do wear vests, this is different. For example, let's say a girl named Penny just started a new job out of college. She makes $40,000 a year, and because she knows a penny saved is a penny earned, she signs up for the 401(k) plan. If she saves 10%, how much does she contribute each year?"

Rusty and Owen had to think about it, but Sandy had the answer right away. "$4,000," she said.

"Very good," said Joey. "Say her company will match 50% of her contributions up to a maximum 3% of her salary. Let's compare those two numbers. What is 50% of her contribution?"

"She contributed $4,000, so fifty percent be $2,000," said Sandy.

"That's right. What is 3% of her salary?"

"She makes $40,000 a year, so 3% is $1,200."

"Correct." Joey was impressed with how quickly she was able to answer his questions. "So you're beautiful and you can do math quickly in your head. What an impressive combination." He smiled at her.

"Thanks, Joey," said Sandy. She began to blush.

"Penny's company will match 50% of her contributions up to 3% of her salary. $2,000 is greater than $1,200, so they will put $1,200 in her retirement account. This is on top of the $4,000 she contributed herself. That's a good deal."

"What about the vest? What color it be?" Rusty pictured a beautiful girl in a brightly-colored vest smiling at him.

"It isn't any color," said Joey. "The vesting period is the length of time she needs to stay at the company in order for her to keep the match money. There are two types of vesting: cliff and graded."

"What's the difference?" asked Sandy.

"A cliff vest means she would have to stay there the full amount of time or she gets nothing. Say her company has a two-year cliff vesting schedule. If Penny quits before working there two years, she gets none of the $1,200 company match."

"What's graded?" asked Sandy.

Rusty answered. "It's where you get an A if you be smart and an F if you be dumb."

Owen responded to Rusty, "It'd be an F for you then."

Joey ignored these comments. "It is where she gets to keep a certain amount after each year. For example on a three-year graded vesting schedule, she would get to keep 33% after the first year, 66% after the second year, and 100% after the third year."

"What about the $4,000 she put in?" asked Sandy.

"She always gets to keep her contributions, no matter what. But to get the company match it takes two years for her to be fully vested."

Rusty said, "I'd rather have Penny be fully un-vested, if you get me drift."

Owen and Rusty laughed.

"You boys be pathetic," said Sandy as she rolled her eyes.

"The funny thing is," continued Joey, "everyone has heard of the 401(k), but not everyone is taking full advantage of it. Many people haven't signed up for it. Others aren't contributing the most they can.

Even more haven't asked about the best way to invest it." He paused. "There's no excuse for knowing about something that can help you, and doing nothing about it."

"I want to do the right thing," responded Sandy. "I just didn't know about the 401(k)."

"I know. You actually seem pretty smart. I wasn't sure about you at first, but now that I know you better, I think you're a high-quality girl."

"Thanks, me hearty. I be impressed with you too."

They smiled at each other for a moment before turning away. For the first time in a long time, Sandy felt butterflies in her stomach.

CHAPTER SIXTEEN

"It be time for a rum break," said Rusty.

"Aye!" Sandy and Owen shouted.

They put away the buckets and brushes and went downstairs to the galley. Owen left the room and came back with a premium bottle of rum. Rusty looked toward where he came from, hoping to find the secret stash, but stopped after Owen unsheathed his blade. They all sat down at the table.

"We should play Hoop 'n Hook!" suggested Rusty.

"Aye!" Sandy and Owen shouted again.

"What is that?" asked Joey.

"It's a game we like to play," said Sandy. She walked over to a drawer and grabbed a pirate's hook. She sat back down, took off her golden hoop earrings and placed them on the table. Owen placed his earring on the table as well. "We take turns holding the hook. Then we challenge someone to throw the hoops onto the hook."

"Like ring toss," said Joey, understanding the concept.

They looked at him with blank faces.

"It's a game landlubbers like to play," Joey said, adjusting himself in his chair. "Anyway, go on."

"Ye get three tries," she said. "For each ring you get on the hook, ye can make someone else take a drink. If you miss all of them, you take the drink." She picked up the three rings. "I be going first, and I challenge you." She placed the rings in front of Joey.

"Ha, okay." Joey picked up the rings.

She held her hand out to the side with the point of the hook facing Joey.

Joey judged the distance to the hook. He felt the weight of the ring. He tried remembering the physics equations from school. He made the motion of tossing a few times. Feeling confident, he tossed the ring. The ring flew over the hook by at least a foot.

They all laughed.

"Hold on," Joey said. "That was my first try." He concentrated on the hook, not taking his eyes off it. He took a deep breath, exhaled, and tossed the ring again. It came within an inch of the hook.

"Better," said Sandy.

He took the last ring. This time he visualized the ring landing in the center of the hook. He spoke encouraging words to himself. He visualized the ring going on the hook again. He tossed the ring. Bulls-eye.

"Well done," said Sandy, nodding her head. "Who do you—"

"You," Joey responded, not letting her finish. He smiled as she took a drink of rum. "I like this game." A thought crossed his mind. "What about my finance lessons? Do you like them? Are they helpful?"

"Aye, matey. They be great," said Rusty. "No landlubber's ever come to teach us pirates anything."

"Do you like being a pirate?" Joey asked.

"Do pirates have wooden legs? I love being on the water. There be plenty of free time to be thinkin' and ponderin'. But what I be liking the best is the freedom. We can sail anywhere and see the world."

This idea hit Joey like a sack of bricks. "I never thought of that. That would be amazing." He thought about all the traveling he wanted to do. "I challenge you, Rusty." He placed the rings in front of him. "Have you been to a lot of places?"

"Do pirates drink a lot of rum?" asked Rusty. "I been to four continents, thirty-five countries, fifty ports, and six hundred bars." He picked up the three rings.

"Wow. Maybe wanting to be a pirate isn't so wacky after all."

"I love being a pirate!" Rusty exclaimed.

"Do you like working for the captain?" Joey asked.

"Do pirates lick their parrots to sleep at night? The captain be the best pirate in the world. Strong but fair. Very cunning. He be a great man. All the pirates be looking up to him." Rusty tossed the first ring. Miss.

"That's good to hear." Joey turned to Sandy. "What about you, Sandy? Do you like being a pirate?"

"Aye. I like being surrounded by nature," she answered.

"Yeah, I never realized how much time I spend inside behind a desk. Pretty unfortunate, now that I think about it. Being in nature sure is nice." Rusty tossed the second ring and it landed on the hook.

"Yo ho!" Rusty yelled. He pointed to Owen. "You drink."

Sandy continued, "I can relax in the sun all day, and I can go swimming whenever me heart desires."

"You swim? I love swimming." Joey remembered going to the public pool and watching the kids play and tell jokes. "That reminds me, what is a pirate's favorite swimming stroke?"

"Don't know," said Sandy.

"A cannon-ball!" Joey laughed. No one else laughed. "Get it? Oh come on, that was funny."

"I think you should be leavin' the comedy to the professionals," said Rusty. He tossed the third ring. Miss. Rusty picked up the rings and put them in front of Sandy.

"I guess I won't quit my finance job yet. Speaking of finance, any other questions?"

"Aye," said Sandy. "Savings obviously be important. How much should me save?"

"That depends on your goal. David Bach wrote a really good book called Automatic Millionaire. In it are guidelines as to how much you should save. He identifies six levels. The first level is dead broke. If you want that, then you shouldn't save, you should spend more than you make, and spend money you don't have on credit cards."

"But I don't want to be dead broke," objected Rusty.

"Okay. The second level is poor. If you want to be poor, then think about paying yourself first, but don't ever actually do it. Live at your means by spending all the money you make. Tell yourself that you will start saving someday."

"But I don't want to be poor, either," objected Rusty.

"Okay, that is good. David Bach's third level is middle class. If you want to be middle class then save five to ten percent of your gross income."

"That be sounding better," said Rusty.

"No it doesn't," said Sandy. "I want to be better than middle class."

Joey nodded in approval. "That is the right attitude to have. If you want to be upper middle class then save ten to fifteen percent of your gross income."

"What if I want to be rich?" asked Sandy.

"Then he says you should save fifteen to twenty percent. And the last level is rich enough to retire early. If you want that, you should save over twenty percent of your gross income."

"Twenty percent?" asked Sandy. "That be a lot of treasure! Not many people are willing to do that."

"You're right, most people aren't," agreed Joey. "And that's why most people aren't rich enough to retire early."

Sandy wondered if she was brave enough to be one of the few willing to save over twenty percent of her income.

"How much should I save?" asked Rusty.

"A general guideline is to save 10% of your income for your 401(k) or IRA. Set it at that and see how it goes," said Joey.

Sandy tossed the first ring. Bulls-eye. "Yo ho!" she exclaimed. She looked at Joey and said, "You drink."

"What if that be too high?" asked Rusty.

"If that's too much and you're struggling, then you can reduce the percentage. Or maybe you find that it isn't that bad and you can increase it."

"How should I invest me retirement savings?" asked Sandy.

"Most companies have someone you can talk to about how to invest your 401(k), either a human resources person or a financial advisor. Ask them. They are there to help to you. Just don't leave it in cash because cash isn't safe in the long-term."

Sandy tossed the second ring. Miss.

"Cash be soundin' safe to me," argued Owen.

"Cash is definitely safe in the short-term. However, cash is actually very risky in the long-term."

"We be pirates. We live for risk and adventure," said Owen.

"But you don't want this kind of risk. When you need this money for retirement in forty years, inflation is going to make things a lot more expensive decades from now. Inflation is why cash is risky in the long-run."

"Argh, inflation," said Owen, thinking about having to pay more for his rum in the future.

Sandy tossed the third ring. Miss. She picked up the rings and put them in front of Owen. "I be working on a pirate ship, matey. We don't be having no HR person or financial advisor. How should I invest me IRA?"

"Before you can invest your IRA, you first need to open one. I encourage you to do your own research, but one good option is opening an account with Vanguard. Vanguard has low expenses, but still ask if they can waive fees for you. The minimum to open an account is only $1,000."

Sandy realized she had saved enough over the years to meet the minimum. She felt pleased. But, she reminded herself, $1,000 was a pittance if she aimed to be a millionaire.

"Call them up, open an IRA, and set it up for automatic contributions from your paycheck. If you want to retire in 2055, put it into the Vanguard Target Retirement 2055 fund."

Owen tossed the first ring. He missed and grunted.

"That's all I have to do?" asked Sandy.

"Basically, if you want the simplest option. Also, make sure your contributions are automatically invested rather than just sitting there in cash. And set it up to automatically reinvest the dividends."

"Can I invest me IRA in gold?" asked Rusty.

"Absolutely. But since you're relatively young, you probably want most of your retirement savings in stocks, both US and international. If you want gold, I would only put around five percent of your total portfolio into it."

Owen tossed the second ring and missed. He slammed his fist on the table.

"But first I be needing treasure to invest. How can I save more money?" said Rusty.

"There are a lot of ways to save and make money. Just Google terms like 'ways to save money', 'money saving ideas,' and 'how to make more money'. This will give you lots of ideas."

"The Google?" asked Rusty, a tremble in his voice. "Do that be the two-hundred-foot tentacled monster of the deep, haunting the Caribbean, lurking in underwater caves and swallowing up ships, pulling them and their crews into the darkest depths of the ocean?"

"No, it's an Internet search engine," said Joey.

"Oh."

"I tried that Google before," said Owen, staring at the last ring in his hand. "It be broken."

"Really? What happened?" asked Joey.

"I be wanting to get rich so I searched the Google. I typed in 'how to grow me booty'. But all it be telling me was about creams and exercises for me bottom. It be broken."

Joey asked, "Your bottom be broken?"

"No, the Google," Owen replied, insulted that his bottom or anything else about him would ever be broken.

"Well, hopefully they can fix it soon." Joey didn't want to talk about Owen's bottom anymore.

Owen tossed the last ring and missed. "Son of a biscuit eater!" he shouted. He took a drink of rum and stormed out of the room.

Rusty picked up the rings and laid them on the table. The three of them continued to chat, tell jokes, and laugh together.

The captain walked downstairs. He was happy to see them getting along. "I see you all be having a good time. Did you learn much today?"

Rusty and Sandy answered emphatically. They talked about what they had learned and what they found to be the most helpful.

"That be good to hear," said the captain. "I need you all to have lots of treasure so I can recruit a bigger crew." He smiled at Joey. "I appreciate you coming here, Giuseppe - I mean Joey. We all be very grateful."

"It's been my pleasure. But there is a lot more to learn."

"Aye, but that be enough for today. Time for some shut-eye." He noticed the rings on table and motioned for Rusty to hold the hook. In rapid succession, the captain tossed the first ring, then the second, then the third. They all landed squarely on the hook. "Yo ho! Yo ho! Yo ho! And that be a drink for each of ya!"

CHAPTER SEVENTEEN

"Land ho!"

Joey awoke to the captain's shout. He ran up the stairs to the main deck and saw land in the distance. "Are we in Boca?"

"Aye," said the captain.

The ship sailed forward and the captain read the riddle again.

The location of the map be hidden outside the mouth of the rat. Inlet the vision of the hidden moon when uttering the creator's infamous words. Venture forth to face and outwit the flowing legless guardians. Expose the path to riches ill-prepared and be cursed for eternity.

Joey looked at the riddle. "I thought Duarte was supposed to be smart."

"He be very smart," responded the captain.

"He said to let in the vision of the hidden moon, but he misspelled 'in let'. It should be two words."

"That do be curious."

Owen came over to them.

"Captain, we be at the tip of Boca. Orders?"

"The riddle says we need to utter Duarte's famous quote, so that's what I be doing," said the captain.

"What quote?" asked Joey.

The captain went to the front bow of the ship, looked out over the ocean, and shouted in a commanding voice, "The sands of the hourglass be stoppin' for no lad. Therefore, don't ignite your cannon tomorrow when ye can ignite it today."

The crew looked all around the water, the land, and the sky. Nothing happened. The captain's heart sank.

"I knew this was a waste of time," mumbled Joey.

"Look!" shouted Rusty.

"What?" The captain rushed over. "You see something?"

"Aye," said Rusty. "Those people on the bridge be waving to us. Ahoy!" Rusty smiled and waved back to the family who appeared to be on vacation.

The captain looked at the family, looked at Rusty, looked back at the family, and shook his head. When he looked at the family again, he saw them standing above a waterway that connected to the Boca Raton Lake. "That be it!" The captain ran down to his quarters. After a minute, he returned holding a map.

The crew gathered around.

"Look, look here. This be the ocean, this be the Boca Raton Lake, and this be a waterway that connects the two. What do that waterway be called?"

The crew started at him blankly.

"The Boca Inlet!" the captain said, his eyes full of excitement. "To the inlet, me hearties!"

The crew jumped up and set course. After careful maneuvering, they steered to the middle of the inlet and in front of the bridge. The captain returned to the bow. Full of confidence, he shouted, "The sands of the hourglass be stoppin' for no lad. Therefore, don't ignite your cannon tomorrow when ye can ignite it today."

They felt a rumble beneath them. The water around the ship began to ripple, and a lightning bolt of water sprang from the inlet to the middle of the ocean. Suddenly, an invisible fog parted, revealing a large island in the shape of a crescent.

"That be it!" shouted the captain with joy. "That be the crescent island, shaped like a moon!"

Joey couldn't believe his eyes. They actually seemed to be on their way to finding the mythical map.

The crew shouted with excitement and hugged each other.

"Onward!" commanded the captain.

They sailed forward to the island. The happiness radiated through the ship for several minutes. However, this elation was quickly curtailed with Rusty's question.

"But, Captain, what about the monster?" Rusty asked.

The crew looked at the captain.

"What monster?" asked Joey.

The captain sighed. "The legend says that the map be guarded by a mythical creature. Most believe it to be a monster. But I think the flowing legless guardian is a mermaid. I got the idea hearing Rusty's joke, and with me research it makes the most sense."

Joey looked at the riddle again. "But the riddle says 'guardians.' It is plural."

"I guess there be two mermaids then." The captain shrugged. "At least I hope that's what it means." He had a worried look on his face.

The crew looked over the ocean, seemingly to look for danger. Their attitude was now more subdued and on guard.

They steered the ship around to the entrance of the bay, which was enclosed by the moon-shaped island. They saw a large cave with a landing dock far in front of them on the other side. Their adventure was off to a smooth start as they sailed into the bay and toward the cave.

About a minute later, Rusty let out a blood-curdling scream. They followed his gaze to behind the ship. Sandy screamed and ran to Joey. He put his arms around her as his eyes widened in fear.

Off in the distance, a sea serpent twice the length of the ship raised its head out of the water. It hissed at them through its long, venomous fangs. The razor-sharp plates protruding from its back shimmered in the sunlight. Its skin was a scaly dark green and its face reminded Joey of a dragon.

"I guess we know why it was plural now," Joey said to himself.

Owen ran to steer the ship, wanting to escape to the open ocean. However, he soon realized that they were surrounded by the island, and the serpent was blocking their only exit. "We be trapped!"

"How we gonna get out of here?" shouted Sandy. "We can't fight that thing!"

The sea serpent bobbed up and down in the water, contemplating its move, getting angrier with each passing second.

The captain looked ahead. "Get to the cave; that be our best hope!" They set the sails for maximum speed.

The sea serpent looked confused at first, but upon realizing their plan, began to race toward them. It slithered through the water quickly.

"It be gaining on us!" shouted Sandy.

The serpent was closing in fast, but as soon as it had appeared, it disappeared. They looked around but couldn't find it.

They closed in on the entrance to the cave. "We almost be there!" shouted Sandy.

A few hundred feet from the cave the serpent reared its ugly head on the side of the ship, water dripping from its fangs as it cocked its head, ready to strike a blow.

"Prepare the cannons!" shouted the captain.

Sandy rushed over to the cannons.

"Fire!" A cannon ball bolted through the air, the blast confusing the beast. Although the canon ball missed its target, the flash and smoke gave the monster enough pause for their ship to sail into the cave. The beast rushed toward the cave but was too big to fit inside. It huffed and puffed, struggling to pursue its prey, but after a few minutes retreated back into the bay.

They docked the boat inside the cave and sat there in shock. After a few minutes of breathless silence, they grabbed the supplies and got off the ship.

The cave was dark except for the sunlight coming in from the entrance. They saw a narrow passageway ahead of them.

The captain looked at the pitch-black passageway and walked toward it. "You all stay here," he said. The rest of the crew sighed in relief.

"I want to come," said Joey. He was as surprised as anyone to hear those words come out of his mouth, but he couldn't resist the temptation.

"I'd be happy to have ya," the captain said with a smile. He turned and squeezed through the narrow, dark passage.

Joey embraced Sandy. Then he took a deep breath and penetrated the darkness, heading into the unknown.

CHAPTER EIGHTEEN

Joey emerged on the other side of the passageway. They lit their torches and found themselves in a small cave. It had a medium-size pool of beautiful blue water in the center, which appeared to be endlessly deep. The water rippled and an object appeared in its depths. It got bigger and bigger, finally breaking the surface and causing splashes all around. The object was a human with beautiful long hair. Actually, not human.

"What do you seek?" asked the mermaid.

Joey's jaw dropped at the sight of her. He couldn't believe a mermaid actually existed.

She had reddish-brown hair that fell to a couple inches above her belly-button. Her lower half was a fin covered in shiny indigo blue scales. Her skin looked well-hydrated and soft. She seemed to be topless, but it was hard to tell since her long hair covered her front side.

Captain Dailey cleared his throat. "I be Captain Rich R. Dailey of the *Prosperous Guardian*. This be me son, Joey. We seek Captain Duarte's treasure map."

The mermaid fluttered around the pool of water. She looked at them skeptically as she circled. "Do you know the story of the great Captain Duarte?" she asked.

"Only parts of it," Joey answered.

The mermaid continued to flutter around, a little slower this time. "Duarte was a legendary pirate who accumulated vast amounts of gold, silver, precious stones and treasure from around the world. He was also a teacher and philosopher. His greatest traits were his cleverness, courage, generosity, and dedication." She paused a moment, either to gather her thoughts or reflect on the man she seemed to have once known.

"He had great pride in his treasure, yet he had no sons to pass it on to." Joey thought he heard sadness in her voice, but she didn't show it. "He felt his treasure was too great for only one man to possess, and he worried about it getting into the wrong hands. Near the end of his life..." again she paused, "he created a map which leads to his famous treasure. He put a curse on the map and gave it to me to guard so only those who are worthy can retrieve it."

The captain stuck out his chest. "We be worthy."

"We shall see." She said this in a way that caused a shiver to run down Joey's spine.

The captain seemed unaffected and ready for whatever came his way.

"You must first answer three riddles to prove your cleverness," she said.

That didn't sound too bad, Joey thought.

"If you answer any incorrectly, you will be turned into mermaids, never to return home again." She smirked as she said it.

Joey gulped. Why did he keep allowing himself to get into these situations?

"Are you courageous enough to continue?" she asked.

Joey turned to the captain to discuss the risk/reward outlook. Before he opened his mouth, the captain said "Aye! We be continuing!"

Joey raised his hands and dropped them. "Well, okay then." He looked down at his legs and moved them up and down to remember the sensation, just in case.

Without waiting, she asked the first riddle. "When you add me to a barrel, I make it lighter. What am I?"

Without hesitation, the captain stared the mermaid in the eyes and said, "A hole."

Joey was impressed that he'd answered so quickly. He looked at the mermaid.

She said, "Your next question is—"

"Wait a second," interrupted Joey. "Did he get it right?"

"Yes, he did," she said without any satisfaction in her voice. "Here is your next riddle. I run but I never walk. I have a bed, but I never sleep. I have a mouth, but I never eat. What am I?"

"I think I know this one," whispered Joey.

"Aye? Tell it to the lady," encouraged the captain.

"Don't you want to hear what I think the answer is first?" asked Joey.

"I be trusting you."

Joey turned to the mermaid. "A river?"

She said, "Your last riddle is..."

Joey felt a rush of relief and joy.

"A clerk at a butcher shop is named Frank. He is five feet ten inches tall, and wears size thirteen shoes. What does he weigh?"

Joey's sense of relief vanished. He turned to the captain. "What does his weight have to do with how tall he is?"

The captain looked back at Joey. "A butcher?"

"A butcher is someone who works at a store and weighs the meat when people order it."

"I know what a butcher be," said the captain. They pondered the question for a few more moments.

"I don't know the answer to this one," said Joey, flexing his leg muscles again.

The captain thought. "Did you say a butcher be weighing meat?"

Joey's face flashed a brightness that lit up the cave. "That's it!" He turned to the mermaid and shouted, "Meat! He weighs meat."

The mermaid's face remained stoic. "Aye, you have shown your cleverness, and you have earned your reward." She swam over to the edge of the water, rolled back a small stone, and revealed the map.

Joey couldn't believe it. He hugged the captain. "We did it! Great job."

The captain smiled and Joey saw years of stress and frustration evaporating from his face. "Thanks," he said.

"Congratulations on getting the map, but remember you cannot unfold the map until you break the curse," said the mermaid.

"What?" exclaimed Joey. "The curse should be broken by answering those riddles."

"No, you have only proved that you are clever and courageous," said the mermaid. "You still need to show your generosity and dedication."

"How do we do that?" asked the captain.

"The map leads to the pieces of eight. Show your generosity by sharing these with your fellow crew. To prove your dedication, one of your fellow pirates must willingly sacrifice themselves to the ocean. Do these things and the curse will be broken."

Joey felt these tasks were impossible. "I don't think I can help with that," Joey said to the captain.

"Actually, Joey," she said, "they cannot break the curse without you."

Joey wanted to ask how that was the case, but she didn't give him the chance. "Open the map before the curse is broken, and you will be forced to rule the dead sea for eternity," she warned.

The captain walked over to the map. He looked in awe at it, savoring the moment. He reached down and picked it up. The cave began to rumble.

"My work is done," she said. "Good luck." She started to dive into the deep water.

"Wait!" shouted Joey. He had many questions, but the most urgent came out of his mouth first. "How are we supposed to defeat the sea serpent?"

"As with the sirens of the past, it is the highest of highs that can bring you to the lowest of lows."

She dove back into the water.

"Wait!" shouted Joey, but she continued swimming deeper and did not return.

The cave continued to rumble and rocks fell from above.

"Let's get out of here," said the captain.

They rushed through the narrow passage to escape back to the large cave, but they found rocks were falling there as well. They saw the crew already on board the ship. Joey and the captain ran aboard, and they set sail.

The narrow passage behind them completely collapsed and the

exit in front of them wasn't far from being next. Rocks landed on the ship, damaging the mast and sails.

"Hold on!" shouted Owen as he steered the ship through the mouth of the cave. They looked behind them and saw the cave collapse a second after their escape. They breathed a sigh of relief.

They turned around, and their relief quickly turned to fear. The serpent was staring at them, its tongue out, hissing at them hungrily. Its eyes widened at the thought of its next meal. It cocked back its head, preparing to strike.

Sandy let out a high-pitched scream. The monster paused but then continued forward, narrowing the gap between them.

"Fire the cannon!" The sea serpent wasn't in the cannon's firing path yet, but the captain hoped the smoke and noise from the blast would scare off the beast again.

Sandy fired the cannon, but it continued slithering forward. It was now next to the ship, its eyes fixed on Joey. The serpent cocked back its head and lunged toward him. Joey dove to the side just as its jaw crashed into the ship, tearing away several wooden planks from the deck as it pulled away. Sandy screamed in a high-pitched tone and the monster backed away.

"That's it," shouted the captain. He ran over to Joey and snatched the dog whistle from his neck. He looked directly at the beast and blew as hard as he could. The monster scrunched its face in pain as it retreated from the ship.

"Good thinking!" shouted Joey.

They steered the ship close to the serpent and aligned the cannons with its position. The captain blew the whistle then yelled, "Fire!"

The sound of explosions and the smell of smoke filled the air as the cannon balls flew toward their target. One of them struck the serpent in the chest, and it fell backward in agony. They continued sailing forward.

When they were halfway out of the crescent island, the monster disappeared under the water. "Ready the cannons!" shouted the captain. The crew was on high alert for its re-emergence.

Without warning, the sea serpent popped out of the water,

its eyes red with anger. Not waiting to cock back its head this time, it sunk its fangs into one of the masts, breaking it in half and bringing the sail down with it. The mast came crashing down toward the deck, heading straight for Sandy. She saw it coming but stood paralyzed in fear. Joey and the captain ran to her. Joey was too late, but the captain pushed her out of the way with a half-second to spare. The wooden mast knocked into the captain, causing him to drop the whistle. It rolled around the deck, and Joey dove after it.

The serpent fixed its eyes on Joey. It opened its jaw and struck at him.

Joey saw its mouth start to close around him. A fang pierced Joey's left leg and he screamed in pain. He grabbed the dog whistle and blew with all his might, causing the monster to back away from the piercing sound. Joey kept blowing, not daring to release it from his lips. The serpent backed away further.

"Fire!" shouted the captain. The cannons blasted, two having a direct hit. The monster fell into the water, causing a huge splash and tidal wave. The wave crashed into the ship, veering it off course. Owen tried to steer it to the entrance of the island, but he couldn't control it due to the damage the ship had taken. The ship was heading toward a series of jagged rocks near the shore. At the last possible second, Owen turned the wheel with all the force he could muster. The ship turned, just clipping the rock formations. Owen breathed a sigh of relief. He steered them through the entrance to the island, and they sailed out into the open ocean.

CHAPTER NINETEEN

The captain looked around. "Everybody be all right?" The crew nodded.

"I've been better," said Joey.

Sandy looked over to Joey and saw him holding his leg, his hand covered in blood from the serpent's fang.

"Sweet Calypso!" She ran to the supply chest and grabbed some bandages. She wrapped up the wound. "There you go. You'll be fine in no time."

"Thanks," he said, smiling at her. He got up and limped over to the side of the ship to join the rest of the crew. The captain patted him comfortingly on his back.

They looked out over the ocean in fear that the sea serpent would reemerge. No one said a word as they stood there on edge. Their hearts beat faster with each shadow they saw in the water. After a few miles, they finally relaxed.

The captain patted Owen on the back. "Nice sailing back there, matey."

"Thanks," said Owen in appreciation.

"Well, that was quite an adventure," said Joey.

"Aye," said Owen. "You better have at least gotten the map."

The captain smiled. He pulled out the piece of parchment from his jacket and showed it to the crew.

They all congratulated him. Owen grabbed for it but the captain snatched it back.

"Why can't I be seeing it?" pouted Owen.

"It's not that easy. The map be cursed," said the captain.

"Yeah, what's going on with that?" asked Joey, annoyed. "Get a pirate to sacrifice himself to the ocean? Nobody is going to do that! Share what's on the map with others? We can't even open it to see what's on it! We can't break this curse."

Owen raised his head. "Aren't you instead supposed to ask, 'how can we break this curse'?" Owen asked sarcastically.

Joey felt embarrassed he hadn't followed his own advice. Owen did make a good point.

"Don't be worrying about that now," said Sandy. "It be time to celebrate getting the map."

"Agreed," said the captain. "You all did a great job helping me get this map. Wait here." He went down to his quarters and came back with a medium-sized bag. "I be appreciating yer work so much, here be a small bonus for each of you." He reached into the bag and handed them several gold coins.

"Thanks, Captain!" said Rusty. "I can be affording that parrot now!"

Joey shot a look at Rusty.

"Or I can be saving it," Rusty said, looking at the ground.

"Aye, thanks, Captain," said Sandy. She turned to Joey. "What should we do with this bonus if we want to be financially responsible?" There were so many things she wanted to do with her money to improve her financial life, she wasn't sure what she should tackle first. "Should I contribute to an IRA for retirement, pay down me debt, build savings, or something else?"

"Great question; a lot of people are confused by that. As I mentioned before, saving $1,000 in your emergency fund should be your first goal. After that, let the interest rates be your guide."

"What do you mean?" she asked.

"Let's take a typical landlubber: he has a 401(k) or IRA, a college loan, credit card debt, and a non-existent emergency fund. Assume the 401(k)/IRA will generate 8% returns over the long term. The interest rate on the college loan is 4%. The credit card charges 17% interest. An emergency fund savings account pays 1% interest. And his company matches 50% of his contributions up to a certain amount. Which one of those should be his top priority?"

Sandy thought about it. "You said let interest rates be your guide, and 50% is the biggest number. So, getting the 50% match?"

"Exactly. Clearly, getting a fifty percent return on your money with the company match is an amazing deal, so that should be his top priority. Once he maxes out his match, then what should he do?"

Sandy thought about the rates again. "He could keep contributing to his IRA and earn 8% over the long term. But he is paying 17% to the credit card company. And seventeen is the next biggest number after fifty. So, pay down the 17% credit card debt?"

"Exactly. Nice work," said Joey.

Sandy felt good about herself. She was actually understanding it.

The captain patted her on the back.

"Using interest rates is a good guide," said Joey, "but it isn't a hard and fast rule. For example, once you pay down your high-interest rate credit cards, you should focus on building three to six months of savings in your emergency fund."

"But a savings account only be paying 1% interest," said Sandy.

"Yes, but it should still be a high priority. The emergency fund is key to reducing financial stress and increasing financial preparedness."

"Should I focus on only one area at a time?"

"No, I don't think so. You can be building your emergency fund, saving for retirement, and paying down debt all at the same time. But don't fund them in equal proportions. Use the interest rate guide to figure out which one of those should get the majority of the money."

They nodded. Sandy asked, "What be a good interest rate?"

Joey thought about this for a second. "Making over a 10% return per year on an investment is pretty good. As for debt, it depends on the kind of debt. Paying over 20% for debt is really high, and a lot of credit cards at retail stores charge 25%, which is insanely high."

The captain looked appreciatively at Joey. "You be giving some solid advice there. Crew, this will help you build your treasure. You be understanding?"

"Aye," they each said enthusiastically.

The captain said, "Understanding and taking action be too different things. Are you actually going to implement what he be saying?"

The crew looked at each other hesitantly.

"Crew?" he asked sternly.

"Aye," they responded.

"Just think when we find the treasure," said Rusty. "We be having enough treasure to do whatever we want! We'll have plenty to invest."

"Aye, but first we need to be figuring out how to open this map." The captain handed the map to Joey. "You hold the map for now. Use it to inspire me crew. Keep teaching them about their finances. You be doing a great job." He turned to walk away. "I need to study me books and journals to figure out how to break this curse. Joey, I want to make sure you can get your majority share of the treasure."

Joey's eyes shot open in surprise.

"Wait, why he be getting a majority share?" Owen asked in anger. "He's only been here for one day; I've been with ye for years."

The captain shrugged. "We can be figuring out all that later. Let's be focused on finding the treasure first." He went off to his quarters.

Owen stormed off, cursing under his breath. Rusty wandered over to the side of the boat. Sandy looked at Joey. "Majority share, aye? You must be excited."

"Of course, who wouldn't be? But I don't want this treasure to cause animosity among the crew. Maybe I'll just give part of my treasure to all of you guys."

"Really? You definitely aren't a pirate."

"Well, Owen is right, I haven't done anything special to deserve an extra piece. I have seen the dark side of money and how it can tear people apart, and in the end it just isn't worth it."

"Rest assured, I'll happily take any treasure you want to give me." She smiled.

"Oh good. I was worried I would have trouble giving away vast fortunes of gold and jewels."

Sandy looked out over the ocean. "When we get the treasure, how should we invest it?"

"That's a great question." A gust of wind swept across the ship. Joey looked down at the map in his hands, nervous he might drop it. "Wait just a second." He went downstairs to the captain's quarters. He opened the door and saw him flipping through a thick manuscript. There were piles of books and articles on his desk.

The captain looked up. "Ahoy, me lad."

"Hi." Joey walked over. "I think this map is safer with you. It's pretty windy up there." He handed him the map.

The captain took the map, looking at it in silence. Then he turned to Joey. "For twenty years, I searched for this map. And here it is. So close, yet so far away." He stared at it with sadness in his eyes.

"You'll figure it out," Joey said with encouragement. "You're a good captain, and you know more about this treasure than anyone. If anybody can figure it out, it's you."

He looked up at Joey and smiled. "I be glad you're here. Thanks for staying."

"I'm glad I'm here too."

"I know it be hard for you being away from work. But I appreciate it, and the crew has been saying great things about you helping them with their finances."

"Honestly, I was dreading coming here. I thought it would be boring and a big waste of time. Little did I know I would end up in the middle of a real adventure."

"Aye." The captain motioned toward the door. "Now get back up there and make me crew rich, aye?"

"Aye, aye, Captain." Joey walked back upstairs and called the crew together.

They gathered around him.

"Crew, Sandy asked a good question. I thought you all would be interested in the answer."

"Why we be needing to continue this finance conversation?" asked Owen. "We found the map, so we're gonna be rich."

"Remember, never count on getting money until it is in your

bank account, or should I say treasure chest," said Joey. "Besides, more money without a base of financial knowledge just leads to more issues."

Rusty nodded.

Joey smiled, then turned to Sandy. "So, what was your question?"

"How should we invest the treasure if we find it?" she asked.

"That first depends on your financial goals. Some people just want to preserve wealth; they don't care about making money, they just don't want to lose it. However, I'm guessing your goal is to save money for retirement."

"Aye," she said.

"There are four main asset classes you can use to make you rich," said Joey.

The crew leaned forward in anticipation.

Chapter Twenty

"The four main assets classes for investing are stocks, bonds, real assets, and cash," said Joey. "You should have part of your money in each."

"What be real assets?" asked Sandy.

"Commodities and real estate," answered Joey.

"Comedies? Ha, they make me laugh," said Rusty.

"Not comedies. Commodities. Oil, corn, aluminum, natural gas, and gold are types of commodities."

"How much should be invested in each?" asked Sandy.

"In general, the longer your time horizon, the more should be in stocks. For example, a twenty-six-year-old saving for retirement could probably have 80% in stocks. The rest could be 10% in bonds and 10% in real assets."

"What about an older person?" asked Sandy.

"If someone is sixty years old and about to retire, they have a shorter time horizon. They may only want 40% of their money in stocks. The rest could be 40% in bonds, 15% in cash, and 5% in real assets."

"I want the flintlock pistol of me favorite captain of the past," said Owen. "It be a classic collector's item. What if I be wanting to save up to buy it next year?"

"If you have a short-term time horizon, like less than a couple years, I would have none of it in stocks. If you want to buy a pistol that soon, just keep it in cash, or invest it in short-term bonds."

"Judging by Joey's recent performance with a pistol, he should be investing in shooting lessons." Sandy winked at Joey.

"Hey!" said Joey, pretending to be insulted. "Past performance is no guarantee of future results." He laughed. "It's not my fault I'm not a master marksman. I never expected to be in a gunfight."

"You're with pirates now, so you best be prepared." She handed him a pistol. "This be a flintlock pistol like the one that Owen wants. It's what pirates from the eighteenth century used."

"But you guys don't use them now?" asked Joey.

"No, they only fire a single shot, and they take too long to reload. But they're good for you to practice with." She tied a rope around an empty barrel and threw it overboard behind the ship. She got close to him and showed him how to load the pistol. He tried to concentrate on what she was saying, but he found it hard given that her body was pressed up against his. Other thoughts filled his mind.

When the gun was loaded, she stood up straight. "Aim at the barrel, and fire."

Joey held the gun out in front of him, feeling nervous. He aimed and fired.

They saw a small splash about ten feet away from the target.

"That be even more pathetic than Rusty's aim," laughed Owen.

Joey bit his tongue and started to load the next round. He began talking finance again to stop them from laughing. "There are many different kinds of stocks. There are stocks of big companies, small companies, companies in the United States, international companies, emerging market companies, etc. There are also many types of bonds. There are treasury bonds, inflation-protected bonds, floating-rate bonds, high-yield bonds, international bonds, etc."

Rusty brought his hand to his forehead. "Now me head be hurtin' more than a wooden leg on fire."

Joey fumbled around with the reloading.

Sandy came over to help. "Weren't you paying attention?"

Joey decided not to answer her question. "I agree, investing can be quite complicated. Luckily, there's an easy solution. They're called target-date funds."

"What do you be knowing about target-date funds? You can't

hit a target to save your life," said Owen with a smirk. He seemed to enjoy putting Joey down.

"Funny," replied Joey. "With target-date funds, you pick what year you want to retire, such as 2055, and put all your money in that fund. The fund company will do all the allocation work for you. They will have more stocks now, and as the years and decades go by, they'll decrease the amount in stocks and increase the amount in bonds and cash."

"Aye, that makes life simpler. Investing be easy," said Rusty.

"Yes, they are good for the beginning investor. However, once you save up a substantial sum of money, then you should consider hiring a competent financial advisor to give you a tailored solution. But until then, target-date funds are a good choice."

"Simple be boring," said Owen.

Joey aimed the gun at the barrel.

"Grip the gun tightly." Sandy grabbed his hand and pressed it together firmly. "Put your feet shoulder width apart." She took her foot and spread his legs. "Control your breathing," she whispered in his ear.

He found himself breathing faster rather than slower, but he tried to focus on the target. He fired. The small splash was six feet away.

Joey turned back to Owen. "You can make investing more complicated if you want. You can use derivatives such as calls and puts. You can invest in hedge funds, which are sophisticated investment vehicles. There is arbitrage, which is both buying one investment and selling short a similar investment. You can invest in straddles or credit derivative swaps." Joey could list hundreds more investment strategies and tools, but figured he would stop there. "But do you know what a pirate's favorite investing strategy is?"

"What?"

"Arrrr-bitrage." Joey chuckled.

Owen looked at him blankly. "I don't get it."

"Never mind," said Joey, again frustrated that they didn't like his jokes. He reloaded the pistol again. He measured the proper amount of gunpowder and poured it down the barrel. The smell of gunpowder filled his nostrils. He took the fifty-caliber ball and wrapped it in a small piece of cotton cloth and put it in the tip of the barrel. He removed the ramrod from below the barrel and used it to push the ball down deep inside. He inserted the ramrod back into the pistol. He added a bit of primer gunpowder near the hammer.

"You said stocks can go down," said Owen. "What if they go down and me investments sink faster than a prisoner tied to the anchor?"

"Believe it or not, because you're young, a sell-off in the stock market can actually be a good thing."

"That be a bunch of monkey feces," replied Owen, waving his hand.

"No. A sell-off lets you buy stocks for cheaper, and you have a long time for them to recover. This is shown with the concept of dollar cost averaging."

Joey aimed the pistol at the wooden barrel bobbing up and down in the calm blue water.

"Close one eye," said Sandy, "and use your other eye to align the sight with the target. Keep your arm straight. Hold it steady. Don't lower the pistol right after you've shot it, rather keep it there to get a nice follow through."

He gripped the pistol tightly. The boat rocked unexpectedly and he fired. He came within five feet of the barrel.

"Dollar cost averaging is where you invest a certain amount of money on a regular basis and buy however many shares you can afford. How much do you plan to put into your IRA each month?"

"200 doubloons."

"Okay, say you invest in the same target-date fund each month. Today that fund costs 20 doubloons. How many shares of the fund can you buy with 200 doubloons?"

Owen said the first number that came to mind. "20."

"No, that's not right. What's 200 divided by 20?"

Owen grimaced. He pondered the question. "10."

"Right. Say over the next few months the fund declines in value and now costs 15 doubloons. Does your 200 doubloons buy more or less shares than last time?

"More," he said.

"That's right. You now can buy 13 shares." He paused. "Say over the next few months the fund rallies to 25 doubloons. Now your 200 doubloons only buys 8 shares."

"Ah, I get it," said Sandy.

"This method has been shown to work quite well over time. This is because you are buying more shares when prices are low and buying less when prices are high. The bottom line is that a sell-off in the market could be good if you have a long time horizon."

Joey reloaded the pistol. The crew thought about the concept of dollar cost averaging for a minute. Rusty didn't understand it, but he felt too embarrassed to say anything.

"What kinds of things can I invest in?" asked Sandy.

"Oh, there are lots of options."

"Do there be any pirate stocks or bonds?"

"Yeah," Owen said. "Pirate bonds be called handcuffs." He smirked.

Joey ignored his joke. "Nowadays you can invest in all kinds of things, especially when using Exchange Traded Funds, or ETFs. ETFs provide over 1,000 themes to invest in."

"What's an ETF? What can I invest in?" asked Sandy.

Joey aimed his pistol again. He adjusted his stance and gripped the gun tightly. He focused on the sight, allowing the barrel to be blurred in the distance. He visualized hitting the barrel. He imagined he was an expert marksman and allowed his body to act as an experienced shooter would. He breathed steadily, cocked the pistol, and fired. He hit the edge of the barrel.

"Nice work!" Sandy gave him a hug.

Joey looked appreciatively at the barrel, then handed the gun back to Sandy. "I didn't know I had it in me."

"Beginner's luck," muttered Owen.

Joey turned his attention back to Sandy. "To answer your questions, an ETF is a basket of stocks wrapped up into one package. For example, the SPDR S&P 500 ETF lets you own the five hundred biggest companies in America. Buying this one ETF is a lot easier than buying those five hundred stocks individually. Its ticker symbol is SPY."

"A tickler symbol?" asked Rusty. "You mean like a feather?"

"No, not a tickler symbol. A ticker symbol. It's the abbreviation for an investment. For example the ticker for Netflix is NFLX. Whole Foods is WFM."

"What's a Netflix and Whole Foods?" asked Sandy.

"Oh, they are popular landlubber companies." Joey grabbed a piece of parchment. "Let's play a game."

"Aye!" exclaimed Rusty. "I be likin' games."

Joey wrote a random list of ETFs and tickers. "Some ETFs have fun ticker symbols. Here's a list of them. Try to match the ticker to the ETF. For example, gold is GLD. The person to match the most wins."

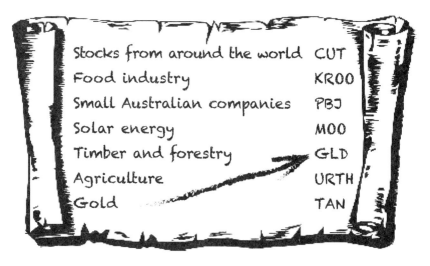

Stocks from around the world   CUT
Food industry   KROO
Small Australian companies   PBJ
Solar energy   MOO
Timber and forestry   GLD
Agriculture   URTH
Gold   TAN

The crew looked over the list.

"Solar energy be TAN!" said Sandy.

"That's right," said Joey.

"The food industry be PB and J," said Rusty as his stomach grumbled.

"Australian companies be K-ROO," said Sandy.

"Agriculture be MOO!" yelled Rusty.

"Timber and forestry be CUT," said Sandy, slapping the wooden ledge in excitement. She looked at the remaining tickers. "Why would stocks from around the world be URTH?"

Owen felt the answer was obvious and said, "Earth."

"Nice work, you guys matched them all," said Joey. He counted the points. "Congratulations, Sandy. You're the winner."

She smiled.

Rusty kicked his foot in disappointment.

Owen acted altogether uninterested.

"So what do I win?" she asked.

"There are lots of things I'd like to give you," Joey said, winking at her.

She giggled.

Owen gritted his teeth.

"If you own several stocks in an account, all of them together are called a portfolio. Here is a sample portfolio. Notice the list of tickers."

JOB   General Employment Enterprises
PLUS   ePlus, Inc.
BEER   Tsingyan Brewery
EQL   ALPS Equal Sector Weight ETF
FUN   Cedar Fair

Sandy and Rusty chuckled at this portfolio.

"Or another possible portfolio is this one."

JOES	Eat At Joe's
HOT	Starwood Hotels & Resorts
AND	Global X FTSE Andean 40 ETF
YUM, MY	Yum Brands, China Ming Yang

"I like that portfolio," laughed Sandy.

"Oh really?" asked Joey, his body shifting toward her.

"Really," she said.

He walked over to her.

Her heart started beating faster.

"I'm glad you like it," Joey said softly.

She ran her fingers through her hair, feeling the tension build.

They looked each other in the eyes, and the environment around them evaporated from their focus. They were drawn into their own world.

Joey put his hand on her lower back and pulled her toward him.

She looked up into his blue eyes and drew in a deep breath.

He put his hand gently on her neck.

Her lips parted slightly.

He moved his lips closer to hers.

She closed her eyes and allowed herself to be drawn to him.

Owen couldn't take it anymore and became infuriated. "That's enough!" he shouted.

Their moment shattered, Joey turned to Owen.

Sandy backed away from Joey.

Owen paced the deck of the ship. "You can't just be satisfied with having your financial life in order and being the captain's favorite? You have to have the girl too? You greedy scum."

"Now hold on," responded Joey. "I came all the way here to teach you how to get your finances in order, and I have taught you a lot so far."

"You haven't taught us what really matters. You don't be telling

124

us the good stuff. I be needing more treasure now! Today! Tell me how to do it."

"You mean like what get rich quick schemes can you do?" said Joey with disdain in his voice. "While it is possible to make a lot of money quickly, it has a high failure rate. Getting rich is an advanced topic, especially when you consider that everyone has a different definition of rich. Either way, before you can tackle bigger challenges you first need to learn the basic concepts of money and understand how to get rich slowly."

Owen became more agitated. "I don't have time for slowly. I need more pieces of eight right now. Not everybody be living a stress-free and debt-free life like you." He paced even faster. Then he stopped. "I be knowing how to get rich quickly. Give me the map!"

Joey looked at him in surprise. "Absolutely not, Owen."

"I may be Owen today, but when I use that map's treasure to pay off me debts and get me own ship, the world will know me by my nickname, Hornigold. I'm gonna become the greatest cutlass-swinging, swashbuckling, shore-pillaging captain the world's ever seen."

"I'm sorry if I misheard you, but did you just call yourself horny gold?" asked Joey, trying to suppress a laugh.

"Benjamin Hornigold be one of history's greatest pirates. He be the first captain of the mighty Blackbeard. He commanded five vessels. He was captain of the thirty-gun *Ranger*, the most heavily armed ship of its day."

"Yeah, but his name was horny gold." Joey smirked as he said the name again.

"His name demands respect!" Owen slammed his fist on the side of the ship. "You don't be knowing nothing about being a pirate, and you don't need that map. Give it to me!"

Joey worried what Owen might do with the map if he got it. "No."

"My time be up. Give it to me now!" Owen drew his sword and pointed it at Joey's stomach.

Chapter Twenty-One

The crew gasped.

Joey help up his hands and walked backward. "Whoa, settle down there, buddy. I don't have the map on me."

"Liar! Give it to me now or face my cutlass." Owen shook his sword at Joey.

Joey stepped back toward the edge of the ship. "I promise, I don't have it," he said, half in fear and half in confusion. Walking backward, his foot hit a ledge. He turned around to discover he was in front of the plank.

Owen smirked upon seeing where Joey stood. "Don't take me for a fool, I be seeing the captain give it to you," Owen shouted as he moved forward with his cutlass.

Sandy drew her pistol and pointed it at Owen. "Leave him alone, Owen."

"Ah, standing up for your boyfriend now, eh?" asked Owen. "Go ahead, shoot me! I know you won't."

She lowered her pistol, frustrated he had called her bluff so quickly. She reached for her sword, but discovered her scabbard was empty.

"You don't understand, I need that map!" Owen said intensely. "Give it to me!"

Joey shook his head, pleading with him. "I gave it back to the captain. I promise! I don't have it on me, buddy."

"I'm not your buddy," Owen said angrily. He swiped his sword at Joey.

Joey's eyes widened in fear as he saw the cutlass heading toward him. He dove off the plank to avoid the blade.

They heard a splash from below as he hit the water.

Sandy ran over to Owen, full of anger. "What did you do?" she yelled, her dagger eyes locked onto him.

The captain ran up the stairs. He looked around. "What's all the racket up here?"

"Owen made Joey walk the plank," shouted Sandy.

The captain looked at Owen, his face full of confusion. "You did what? Lower the rowboat! Don't let me son drown!" He ran over to the side of the ship. He spotted Joey swimming toward a small island. "Wait, he be fine. He still be a good swimmer." He breathed a sigh of relief. He turned back to Owen. His face became cold with anger.

Owen stood there defiantly, arms crossed. "He deserved it. We don't be needin' Joey anyway. We can become great without him."

The captain couldn't believe his ears.

"Owen demanded the map from him," said Sandy.

The captain's eyebrows narrowed. "What'd you want the map for?"

Owen looked away. He said nothing.

"What were you gonna do with the map, Owen?" the captain asked sternly. He walked toward him.

Owen lowered his head, uncrossed his arms, and put his hands in his pockets.

The captain stared at him, not saying a word, waiting for Owen to answer.

"I..." Owen struggled with what to say. "I got myself into a bit of trouble."

"What kind of trouble?"

Owen was silent. Then he answered, "Financial trouble."

The captain took a step back. "And did you be askin' Joey about it?"

Owen crossed his arms again. "No, I don't be wantin' his help."

The captain stomped his food on the ground. "You and your stubbornness! That be a barnacle brain thing to say. He came all the way to help you."

Owen stood there steadfast, avoiding the captain's gaze.

"I don't care what you want," said the captain. "Quit being stubborn and ask Joey for help. That's an order." He stripped Owen of his cutlass, then looked at the broken mast and the other damage to the ship. "We be having plenty of repair work to do here, so we've got some time. Get going." He motioned toward the plank.

Owen looked at the captain, at the plank, then at the captain again. "What? I'm not walking the plank!"

The captain gave him a stare that made Owen move toward the plank against his will.

"Oh, yes, ye be walking it," said the captain as he walked toward him. Owen backed up as he did. "You clearly be having issues with me son, so don't be coming back until you resolve them. Beg for forgiveness if you have to. Work it out, 'cause if you ever be pullin' anything like that again, you're off the crew."

Owen had involuntarily walked onto the plank.

"And kiss your share of the treasure goodbye. Argh!" The captain lunged forward, causing Owen to fall from the plank and into the water below.

CHAPTER TWENTY-TWO

O wen started swimming to the small nearby island. He thought about his actions. Hitting the cold water had cooled off his anger. Gradually he came to the realization that his temper and jealousy had gotten the better of him again. Joey hadn't done anything wrong. Owen made the decision to be a little nicer to Joey. Maybe if he opened up to him about some of his financial stress, they could find common ground. As he got closer to shore, he became more confident in his ability to smooth things over with Joey and looked forward to patching their differences.

He got to shore and adjusted his eye patch. Joey was sitting on the beach. "That be quite a swim, aye?" Owen asked Joey, forcing a smile.

Joey looked over and saw that Owen didn't have his sword. He got up and stomped toward him, his face full of anger. "What was that about?" Joey yelled at Owen. "You think you can push me around?" Joey shoved Owen back into the water.

Owen felt his blood begin to boil. But he tried to remain calm and control his temper. "I be sorry about me actions back there. I have trouble controlling me temper."

"You think?" Joey shouted in his face. "You pull anything like that again and I'll poke out your other eye!"

"Poke out me eye? Me eye be just fine." He lifted his eye patch to show a perfectly functioning eye.

This caught Joey off guard. He stepped backward. "What's with the eye patch then?" he asked with an accusatory tone.

"Us pirates need to be moving quickly from above deck to below deck, especially when raiding an enemy ship. If me eyes are used to bright sunlight and I move below deck, it could take twenty-five minutes for me eyes to adapt to the darkness. But if I always keep a patch over me right eye, I just switch the eye patch to the left eye and me right eye be ready for the dark."

Joey stared at the patch. "Whatever, that doesn't excuse you from acting like a jerk earlier. I won't tolerate being treated that way, especially when I am here trying to help you guys."

"Aye, matey. Me apologies. I be under a lot of stress right now, and that map can get me out of trouble. Then I be seeing you and Sandy about to kiss, and you mocked me nickname. I became overwhelmed by it all and lost me temper."

"Yeah, I could tell," scoffed Joey.

Owen hesitated before saying, "I be in a bit of financial trouble."

"Well, I'm sure you can figure it out," said Joey, uninterested in his problems.

"I be in trouble with debt, matey. And my deadline be up."

Joey remembered Ivan mentioning a deadline during their bar fight. "Deadline for what?" asked Joey, the hairs on his neck rising.

"To pay back the debt," Owen said cautiously.

"Owen, who did you borrow money from?" he asked sternly.

"Quite a few people. Sandy. Rusty. The hat shop. The sailing instructor shop."

"Anybody else?"

Owen paused and looked away.

"Owen?" he asked again, more firmly this time.

"And, Captain Goodman."

"You took a loan from Captain Goodman?" Joey exclaimed. "What were you thinking!"

"I was desperate, matey. I already borrowed from everyone else. And all the banks rejected me, saying I don't be having a good credit score. I don't even be knowing what a credit score is, but I want to cleave it to the brisket."

"The deadline is today?"

"No, yesterday. I now be officially late."

"Do you have the money?"

"No."

"What can they do to punish you?"

"Whatever they want." Owen's shoulders slumped and he put his hands in his pockets. Reluctantly, he swallowed his pride and asked, "Can you help me?"

Joey was taken aback by his question. "I don't know. After the way you treated me..."

"I be sorry about that. Can we start over? I'm not a mean person, I just be in a rough spot. I could really use yer help." Owen looked at him, half with fear and half with puppy-dog eyes.

Joey felt Owen might actually be sorry for his actions. "I guess so. But don't think of pulling anything like that again."

"Aye, cross me heart I won't."

"So you have a lot of debt." Joey remembered what Owen had said earlier. "Once we find the treasure, that shouldn't be as big of an issue."

"No, matey." Owen shook his head, mad at himself. "Our captain said because of what I did, I don't get any of the treasure."

"Oh." Normally Joey would feel sorry for him, but he didn't at the moment. "Why did you get into so much debt in the first place? Do you have a spending addiction?"

"All me expenses have been for learning to become a captain. I'm gonna be a great captain one day."

"Right, you've mentioned that."

"I be needin' to earn more treasure to pay off me debt."

Joey sat in the sand, getting comfortable for a long talk. Owen joined him.

"I know that you think more money is the answer, but actually more money usually just leads to more debt. Having more money only helps if you change your money habits first. Just look at all the bankrupt lottery winners. Do you know where your money is going?"

"It be disappearing faster than a ship in the Bermuda Triangle."

"There are a few steps to getting out of debt. The first step is to stop digging."

Owen shook his head at this. "No. Never."

Surprised, Joey asked, "Really? Why?"

"Telling me to stop digging for treasure be like me telling you to stop being a landlubber. It'll never happen."

Joey thought about this comment. "Well, I don't know. The more time I spend out here on the water and in nature, the more I like it. But I didn't mean you have to stop digging for treasure. I meant stop getting into more debt. The way to do that is to spend less than you make. Okay?"

"Aye aye, Captain."

Joey smiled at the thought of being a captain. He actually liked the sound of it. "Okay, the next step is to try lowering your interest rates."

"How?"

Joey reached for a pile of sand and let it fall through his fingers. He watched the sand sparkle in the sunlight as it fell. "I'm not sure what kind of debt you have. Typically a landlubber could refinance their home mortgage or look into getting a lower rate on their car loan from a bank."

"I don't have a house or a car. But I be having a credit card."

"You can call your credit card company and politely ask for a lower rate."

"Ha. That wouldn't work."

"Oh really, you've tried it?"

"Argh, no."

"That's a problem with non-wealthy people. They get advice about ways to save or make money, and they just assume it won't work. Before dismissing every idea, why not research the idea first?"

"But nine out of ten times it's usually too good to be true, or a scam."

Joey grabbed a pile of sand again. As the sand fell from his hand, it revealed a seashell. He realized it was a king's crown seashell, and he admired its beauty. "That might be true. But what if it is actually that amazing opportunity you've been hoping for? You won't know unless you investigate."

Owen nodded.

Joey continued, "Non-wealthy people have the mindset that they will always be poor, and they don't try anything to change it. Wealthy people, on the other hand, have the mindset that they are destined to be rich. They keep trying everything until they find a way that works."

"I never thought about it like that before," said Owen. "Alright, I'll try everything you tell me, just to see for meself how it works. What be the next step for getting out of debt?"

CHAPTER TWENTY-THREE

Joey and Owen decided to walk the beach around the island.
"The next step is the debt snowball method. It is a technique that has been taught by many financial professionals for years," said Joey.

"What be a snowball?"

"Snow is like soft frozen rain. Picture a ball of snow rolling down the hill. The ball starts small, then slowly it gets bigger, and bigger until it becomes a large and powerful force."

"Aye, that be makin' sense. I had a kidney stone that kept getting bigger like that. You should call it the Kidney Stone Method."

Joey hoped the unpleasant visual in his mind would go away soon. "Thanks for the suggestion, but I think I'll stick with the snowball method. Basically, this is where you start with your smallest debt and you pay that off first. Then you take the money you were paying on that small bill and put it toward the next smallest bill until it gets paid off. You continue doing this until all your payments snowball into a large payment that knocks down your bills quickly."

"I don't be understanding. I thought you were supposed to pay off your debts with the highest balances first."

"No, that is definitely wrong. The best way is to pay off the debt with the highest interest rate first. Mathematically speaking, it will save you the most money."

"So why not do that instead of the Kidney Stone Method?"

"Because humans are emotional creatures who like instant

gratification. I have found that the snowball method is more satisfying, and people are more likely to stick with it. If you have enough self-control to do the highest interest rate method, then do that. But many people end up quitting because it isn't as emotionally satisfying."

As they continued walking around the island, they saw a light shimmer in the bushes. Owen walked over to investigate.

"What is it?" asked Joey.

"A shovel." Owen pulled it out and showed it to him, then noticed some foliage on the ground. He picked up the branches and foliage. What they found underneath made them excited. There was a series of rocks that were strategically placed on top of loose sand. They were in the shape of an X.

"What do you think?" Joey asked. "X marks the spot?"

"I don't know, matey. It almost seems too easy."

"Do you think there's treasure under there?" asked Joey excitedly.

"Probably not, but you said it yourself, it be worth finding out. I could use some pieces of eight." Owen started digging.

"What are pieces of eight? I've heard the term before but don't remember what it means."

"Treasure. They be the Spanish dollar coins from the sixteenth century, made of gold and silver. They can be cut into eight pieces of bits, hence the name."

"Interesting."

"So how would I do the Kidney Stone Method?"

Joey was about to correct him on his terminology but figured he was wasting his breath. He looked in the bushes and found another shovel. He helped Owen dig, hoping that they would find buried treasure. "What debt do you have?"

"I be having seven debts."

"How much do you owe Captain Goodman?"

"5,000 doubloons."

Joey whistled. "Well, that is a good chunk of change. But it isn't hopeless. Since that is a special situation, let's focus on putting a plan together for the other debt first."

"Aye."

"Ignoring Captain Goodman's debt, how much do you owe, and what are the minimum monthly payments?"

Owen tried to remember. "I be owin' Sandy 210 doubloons, and she wants at least 15 doubloons each month as a minimum payment."

"I'm sure she reminds you of your debt all the time."

"Aye, and she tries to make me scrub the poop deck for her." He clenched his fist. "I owe 500 doubloons to Rusty and he wants 25 doubloons each month. I owe 890 doubloons to the hat shop for 38 a month. I be owing 2,800 doubloons to the sailing school with a monthly payment of 92 doubloons, but I haven't been able to pay that in a few months."

"Now I understand why Mr. Saylors chased you out of his shop."

Owen nodded. "On me credit card I owe 6,100 doubloons for 175 a month. I've got the Gold Card."

"Of course you do. Anything else?"

"Yar, me education loan. I owe 19,100 doubloons for 195 a month."

"You went to college?" Joey was impressed.

"Aye, me lad, at the best school in the land."

Joey was even more impressed. "Where did you go?"

"I went to The Goonies School of Swashbuckling and Piracy," he said proudly.

Joey decided to refrain from commenting on his college choice. "Okay. Your smallest debt is to Sandy. Paying 15 doubloons per month will pay it off in seventeen months. You may have noticed that 210 divided by 15 per month equals 14 months. So you would think it would take 14 months to pay it off, but in reality it takes 17 months. Why do you think that is?"

"I don't know, matey," said Owen as he continued to dig.

"It's because the credit card company is still charging interest while you're paying down the balance. If they charged you zero interest, then it would only take 14 months. But as you pay down the debt, they keep adding interest for what you still owe. That's why it takes 17 months to pay off. This is true for all debt."

"They be acting like greedy buccaneers," snarled Owen.

"Yup, that's why it is better to have no debt. But that advice doesn't help you now. You have six bills we are looking at. The minimum payments for all of them add up to 540 doubloons per month." Joey took out his cell phone. It was still wet from the swim, so he was thankful he got the water-proof case before this trip. He typed in Owen's balances and minimum payments.

DEBT	BALANCE	MONTHLY PAYMENT
Sandy	210	15
Rusty	500	25
Hat Shop	890	38
Sailing School	2,800	92
Gold Card	6,100	175
Goonies School	19,100	195
Total	29,600	540

"Making the minimum payments, it would take you 130 months to become debt free. Over that time period, you would pay 7,716 doubloons in interest to the banks and credit card companies. I don't know about you, but I would rather pay that money to myself."

Owen agreed.

Joey wiped his brow, which was beginning to sweat. "The snowball method lets you get debt free faster without having to make any extra money. Let me ask you, when you pay off Sandy's loan, what are you going to do with the 15 doubloons per month you don't have to pay anymore?"

"I don't know, probably drink and piss it away."

Joey smirked. "I like the honesty. Let me show you a better way."

CHAPTER TWENTY-FOUR

This is how to use the snowball method," said Joey as they continued to dig. "Instead of wasting those 15 doubloons per month once you pay back Sandy, put it toward your next smallest debt, which is what you owe Rusty. Paying that additional 15 doubloons per month will pay back Rusty in only five months."

"I be liking that. I want to pay them back soon. Things haven't been the same between us since I had to borrow money from them."

"Yeah, I have the philosophy that you don't lend money to friends and family. If they need money, just give it to them as a gift and don't expect to ever get paid back. Having a healthy relationship is more important than the money."

"Aye. I be realizing that's true now."

Joey paused from his shoveling to pull on his shirt rapidly a few times, trying to cool himself. "When you pay back Sandy and Rusty, you will have an extra 40 doubloons per month. Your next smallest debt is the hat shop. How much are you paying them?"

"38 doubloons per month."

"Well, if you add in the 40 doubloons that you will no longer need to pay to Sandy and Rusty, you can pay the hat shop 78 doubloons per month. Keep repeating this process and eventually you will have the full 540 doubloons per month ransacking and pillaging your biggest debt, the education loan. This is called the snowball method."

"That sounds great, matey. But do it work?"

"Let's see." Joey typed some numbers into his cell phone.

"Rather than becoming debt free in 130 months, you'll be debt free in 65 months. That is less than half the time."

"Saving time be good," said Owen as he continued to shovel.

"Saving money is even better. Rather than paying over 7,700 doubloons in interest, you pay only 5,200 doubloons. This is 2,500 doubloons in savings. How would that make you feel?"

"Better than a powder monkey hornswoggling the hempen halter," said Owen.

Joey scratched his head. "I'll assume that's a good thing. Anyway, you accomplished all that without needing any extra money. No extra hours at work required."

"That be the best part," he said.

"Just imagine how much faster you would become debt free if you paid more than the 540 doubloons minimum per month."

Owen looked confused. "Why would I want to pay more than I have to?"

"Let me tell you a story about my cousin. One day she was feeling sad, so she decided to go on a shopping spree. She bought $1,000 worth of clothes and makeup at the department store. She went to the checkout and the nice lady asked her if she wanted to save 10% by signing up for the store credit card."

"Aye, that be happening to me too. Did she do it?"

"Yes, she signed up. After all, it sounds like a good deal, right?" Owen nodded.

"A few weeks later the bill came. Since she had other expenses, she just made the minimum payment. She set it up to automatically pay the minimum each month and basically forgot about the bill. Guess how many months it took her to pay it off?"

"In honor of the pieces of eight, I guess eight months."

"Nope."

"Fourteen months?" he guessed again.

Joey shook his head. "Try one hundred and fifty-six months."

Owen's jaw dropped.

"That's right, thirteen years. By the time it was over, she paid $2,100 for $1,000 worth of stuff. And she doesn't even wear the clothes anymore. Like I said, paying the minimum doesn't make any sense."

"Aye, matey, making the minimum payments be for swabbies."

Joey shielded his eyes from the bright sun. The heat became overbearing, so he took off his shirt. Then he continued to dig. "As for your situation, let's say you pay an extra 50 doubloons per month toward your debts. Under the normal snowball method you would pay back Sandy in 17 months."

"How long would it take if I be paying the extra 50 doubloons per month?"

"You'd pay her back in 4 months."

Owen nodded in approval.

Joey continued, "Rather than paying off the sailing school in 32 months, you'd pay it off in 24 months. And you become debt free a half year earlier. How would you like to be debt free that quickly?"

"That be sounding very good." Owen shoved the shovel down into the sand and heard a clank.

"And that is sounding very good," said Joey.

Owen got down on his hands and knees. He scooped out the sand that was in the way. Joey got down and helped him. They reached deep into the sand.

"I feel a handle," said Owen.

"Me too," said Joey. They looked at each other, eyes open wide with excitement. They pulled up on the handles at the same time. The sand fell down like a waterfall around the container as they pulled it out. They wiped off the sand and revealed a treasure chest.

"Well, what do you know?" said Owen as he looked at the prize. The chest was made of dark wood, had a rounded top, and had a big lock on the front of it.

"We actually found buried treasure!" exclaimed Joey, patting Owen on the back.

"Aye. Now we be needing to figure out how to open it."

Joey shrugged. "Maybe we can slam a big rock against it."

Owen examined the lock. "Aye, that could work."

Joey looked to the ocean. To his surprise, he saw their ship sailing away. "Hey, why is the captain leaving us here on the island?"

Owen looked. "They be testing out the sails to see if the repairs be working. They'll be back soon."

"Oh, okay."

They left the treasure chest to explore the island for a rock.

"I like the Kidney Stone Method, but it still be taking a long time to get debt free," said Owen.

Joey looked at him, confused. "How can you be thinking about that when we just found buried treasure?"

"I be skeptical of that chest we found. As you said, I'm not counting on any treasure until I hold it in me hands."

"Good point." Joey was pleased Owen was heeding his advice. "And yes, even with these techniques it can take years to become debt free. That's why it's better to never have debt in the first place." He paused. "But that advice is too late for you," he said, his voice trailing off.

"Aye," said Owen, scowling. "I wish I knew earlier about avoiding debt. The short-term pleasure don't be making up for the long-term pain."

They saw a large rock up ahead.

"Since it can take years to get out of debt," said Joey, "it's important to remember that you can have fun and be happy while paying it down. People think they have to be unhappy while paying down debt, but that's not true at all. Some people are the happiest they have ever been when paying down debt."

"Really?"

"Yes, because they are less stressed, and it feels good to see their balances decrease. Plus, don't forget that the best things in life are free."

"Aye, matey. It be costing nothing to pillage another ship."

They picked up the rock together and walked it back to the treasure chest.

"Um, I guess so. Also, you should reward yourself along the way. After each debt you pay off, take a month's worth of the extra snowball money to buy something nice for yourself."

"I be liking that idea." Owen agreed that it would be impossible to be on such a restrictive budget for years and years. Rewarding himself along the way sounded like a great idea to make it work.

"But can I get debt free even faster?"

Joey pondered his question. "You could temporarily cut some of your monthly expenses. For example, a landlubber could cancel their cable, cell phone, and Internet service for a few months to put that money toward their debt."

"But there be a limit to how much you can be cuttin'."

"You're absolutely right. That's why a better way to get out of debt it is to increase your income. You can never go wrong with increasing your income, as long as you do it in an ethical way. As a warning though, when you increase your income make sure to keep your expenses the same. Don't increase your expenses when you make more money or you'll feel just as poor as before."

They got back to the treasure chest. Owen pounded the rock against the lock for two minutes. Finally, it broke and fell off.

"That be pretty easy," said Owen. "You ready to open it?"

"Aye, aye!" exclaimed Joey.

They opened the treasure chest and felt themselves being lifted in the air. They quickly realized that a net had been hidden under the sand, and they were now trapped in it, hanging from a tree.

"I knew finding that treasure be too easy," said Owen, banging his hand against the net.

"It looks like we're in a bit of trouble," said Joey.

"Aye. But I can figure a way out of this; just give me a few minutes."

"I like the positive attitude," said Joey.

Owen wrangled with the net. He was making progress. Then he glanced at the ocean and stopped moving. His face turned white.

Joey looked in the same direction and saw a pirate ship heading straight for them. "Whose ship is that?"

Owen didn't respond. He put his face in his hands.

"Owen, whose ship is that?" Joey asked emphatically, afraid to hear the answer.

Owen said in despair, "Captain Goodman."

CHAPTER TWENTY-FIVE

Captain Goodman's ship arrived. A woman with striking looks stepped onto the island. She was in her late twenties, with a hard face and long dark hair. She wore a revealing purple dress.

Two crewman who Joey didn't recognize followed her off the ship, both wearing purple bandanas. One wore a gold medallion and was in good shape. The other man was frumpy and slightly overweight.

"Look who we be catching trying to steal our treasure." The woman ordered the crew to cut them down.

Joey and Owen fell eight feet and hit the ground with a thud.

Joey rubbed his sore arm after the fall. He didn't know who she was or what she wanted. He looked at the ship but didn't see anyone else coming. "Who are you?" asked Joey.

The woman smiled. "I be Anita Goodman."

Joey was shocked. He had assumed Captain Goodman was a man.

"Surprised, aye? I suppose these sons of biscuit eaters didn't tell ya anything about me, did they?" Her eyes narrowed as she glared at Owen. "Figures."

Ivan came running off the ship and onto the island, full of fury. "Good, we got them! Let's cut them into little pieces and feed them to the sharks." Joey could tell he meant it literally by the tone of his voice. Ivan rubbed his eye patch as if it was causing him pain. "They be trying to blow us up with cannons, we caught 'em stealing our treasure, and this barnacle brain be late paying us back what he borrowed. What we be waiting for?" he exclaimed.

Anita examined her prisoners. "Good point," she said as she motioned to Ivan. "Kill them both." She turned to walk back to her ship.

"Wait, no!" shouted Joey.

She didn't stop. Ivan drew his sword, his blood-thirsty eyes filled with eagerness.

"Come back, I can explain!" Joey shouted with more urgency.

She continued walking, ignoring Joey's pleas. Ivan walked toward them and lifted his sword above his head, ready to strike. Owen tore at the net, trying to escape.

In desperation Joey yelled, "We found Duarte's treasure map!"

She stopped. "Hold," she commanded Ivan.

In frustration, Ivan threw his sword on the ground, kicking the sand.

She walked over to Joey. "What did you say?"

"I said we found Duarte's treasure map," he said reluctantly.

She tried to comprehend what he just said, but she couldn't believe it. "Prove it."

"You know we had the riddle, right?" She nodded. "We figured out the location, Boca Raton. We went there, revealed the crescent island, battled the sea serpent, and convinced the mermaid to give us the map."

Her eyes opened wide. "I knew it be a sea serpent. Captain Dailey never listened to me." She held out her hand. "Give it to me."

Joey hesitated. "We don't have it."

"Ah," she said. "I guess you be out of luck." She drew her sword.

"Leave him alone!" said Owen.

She rushed over to Owen. "Shut your trap. You're already a dead man. You missed your deadline."

"But I can give you the map for my payment," said Owen hurriedly. "It'll more than cover the late payment. I just need to get it from Captain Dailey."

She squinted at him. "You think I'm gonna let you walk away from here? And you think the captain is going to give up his map for you?"

She shook her head. "No, not for a sorry pirate like you. Your debt be past due, and you have no way to pay." She turned to Ivan. "Kill him."

Ivan smiled and picked up his sword. Owen looked around desperately for any weapon he could use in defense.

A shot of adrenaline rushed through Joey. He thought hard about how he could save Owen.

Ivan walked over, toying with Owen. He pretended to stab Owen a few times, taunting him. Ivan lifted his sword.

"Wait," said Joey. "Take me as collateral."

"Collateral?" she asked.

Ivan stood there, eyes wide and sword raised, waiting for the command.

"Yes," continued Joey. "Take me as a prisoner, and you can use me to secure Owen's loan. The captain won't let anything happen to me, so you can be confident you will get your payment."

Anita shook her head. "Why do he care about some landlubber like you? Go ahead, Ivan."

Ivan pulled back on his sword like a spring, ready to swipe at Owen's head.

"Because I'm his son!" shouted Joey.

She looked at Joey, examining him from head to toe. "Giuseppe?" An evil smile crossed her face. "Lower your sword, Ivan."

Ivan threw his sword on the ground again, cursing.

She walked up to Joey. "Aye, his precious son. Yes, he would do anything for you." She turned to Ivan. "Tie Owen up to the tree. He can tell the captain that if he wants to see his son alive again, he better deliver the map to me by midnight. After midnight, Giuseppe be discovering firsthand about Monbars the Exterminator's favorite form of torture."

Joey gulped.

"Time to go," she said. "We be needing to prepare the ship for Captain Dailey. Grab him." She motioned to Joey.

Ivan spat on Owen. Then Ivan grabbed Joey's shirt off the ground, threw it at him, and dragged him onto the ship.

Owen struggled to get out of his binds, but could only watch as they sailed away.

⚔ ⚔ ⚔

"Get in the cell," the crewman commanded in a particularly nasty tone. He motioned for Joey to enter the jail cell below the deck of Anita's ship.

"Fine," said Joey. He looked around the prison room. It was dark, grimy, and had a bad smell. The floor and walls were covered in dirt and soot. The room was empty except for a large chest and a chair.

The crewman locked the cell. Joey noticed he was wearing an ornate gold medallion with an intricate design. It had a hypnotizing effect on Joey. "What is that you're wearing?"

"A gold medallion from Incan times."

"That looks really cool." Joey felt himself being drawn to it. "Can I see it?"

The crewman gave Joey a disgusted look. "Touch me loot, feel me boot."

"Fine then," Joey said. "No need to be rude."

The crewman scoffed. "You'd be the same way if ye worked for her."

They heard footsteps coming down the stairs.

"Here she comes," said the crewman. He added under his breath, "That foul wench."

Anita came into the room and looked at the crewman. "Get out of here, ya son of a biscuit eater. I need to spend some time with me new guest."

The crewman left, mumbling obscenities.

"Welcome to yer new home, ye scurvy dog. This be me ship, the *Fortuitous Dagger*." She looked around the room. "I have many good memories of this here ship, been renting her now for almost a year."

"Rent?" asked Joey. "Why don't you buy one?"

She looked offended. "What business be it of yours? Besides, you be needing lots of treasure to buy a ship." She waved her hand dismissively. "What do you know about money? I don't be needing to waste me breath on you."

It was Joey's turn to look offended. "Actually, I know a lot about money. A lot more than you," he said defiantly. "I have been studying it for years and work on Wall Street."

She looked at him, intrigued. She paced back and forth, seeming to ponder something. She became excited and walked back and forth faster. She then stopped, as if a light bulb had gone off in her head. She turned to him. "So you can help me buy a ship? And quickly?"

"Maybe," he said. "Why do you need it quickly?"

She frowned at this question, then turned away. After a moment she replied, "Because me dream ship is about to be bought by someone else. A wretched man. I be wanting to get it before he does."

"Why do you need a new ship in the first place? This ship seems to be fine."

She became irritated by his questions. She again hesitated before answering, as if trying to think of what to say. "It ain't about the ship, ye grog-snarfing blowfish. It be about what a fancy new ship can get me. Something me wanted for too long..."

Knowing her reputation for destruction and punishment, he guessed, "Something that can give you entertainment, like a new plank?"

She slammed her fist on the table. "Don't ever be saying that word again!"

Confused, he asked, "What did I say?" He couldn't imagine a pirate never saying the word "plank".

Calming herself, she said, "You saying that brings back painful memories, memories of me ex-boyfriend. His name be Jack 'The Long Plank' Johnson. He ran off with a despicable wench and I never be seeing him again."

Joey scratched his head. "You have such a scary reputation. I'm surprised to see you have an emotional side."

"I be a good person at me core." She gazed into the distance, as if reflecting on a painful memory. "Others don't know what I went through. People don't be understanding me, and I don't owe them any explanation."

"You're a successful pirate. I'm sure there are plenty of guys who would love to be with you."

"Aye, and they all be blowfish snorters. I be needing a good man, like Jack was before his betrayal. I can get the men I don't want, but can't get the men I want. That's why I be building me reputation for ruthlessness."

Joey was confused. "You think being a ruthless pirate will get you high-quality guys?"

She had a smug look on her face. "Men love a mean and dominant woman who keeps 'em guessing. Men like it when they're not sure if they'll get a soft kiss from ya, or a dagger in the stomach. It forms an emotional bond that can't be replaced, and keeps things exciting and unpredictable."

Joey was familiar with many dating theories, but he had never come across this kind of logic before. "Who told you that?"

"Me mother. She read the book *Why Men Marry Witches* or whatever it be called. She said I lost Jack because I be too nice. Well, I'm not making that mistake again. Now I be the meanest pirate the world seen in a long time."

Joey felt her theory didn't make any sense. But there had been many crazy theories in the past, and some of those ideas ended up changing the world. He believed in not judging something until learning whether it produced results. If a dumb idea produced impressive results, then it wasn't a dumb idea. "How's that going for ya?"

"I still don't have a man," she said softly.

Upon hearing that, he felt he was justified in thinking it was a dumb idea. "Do you think you should revise your ideas?"

"Aye, that's what I be doing."

Joey admired that she was changing a losing strategy, even though she was emotionally attached to it.

"What I be doing isn't working, so it be clear to me that I need to be even meaner."

Joey shook his head. He sat down on the stool in his cell.

"What you be doing?" she asked. "There be work to do. You're not staying in there." She unlocked the cell and put handcuffs on him. "Do you really be knowing about money?"

"Yeah," he replied.

"For me new ship, I don't have enough doubloons to pay for the twenty percent down payment," she said. "What can I do?"

He pursed his lips and crunched his nose. "Why should I help you? I don't take kindly to being kidnapped."

She pondered this comment. "What do you want?"

He thought it over. "If I help you get your ship, you let me go."

She gave an evil snicker. "Why do you want to leave? Ye seem to be a smart lad. Join our crew."

Joey was repulsed by the idea. "I would never become a pirate as long as there are deplorable buccaneers like you sailing the seas."

"I be the only one as deplorable as me, I can assure you that," she said proudly. "All those other pirates follow the Code, and I most certainly do not. But your offer intrigues me."

"So do we have a deal?" he asked hopefully.

She was torn on this decision. She didn't want to let him go, but she really needed the ship right away. She pondered it more, and an evil grin flashed across her face. "Aye, you have a deal."

Joey felt relieved. He was confident that he could help her get her ship, and then he was free to go. But he had a nagging suspicion that she agreed too easily. "Wait a second," he said. "The deal is that you let me go, unharmed."

She smiled. "Ah, don't you be the smart one." His new stipulation foiled her previous idea. She thought this over as she tapped her chin. "Aye, unharmed. Do we have a deal?"

Joey was thrilled with the deal, but he played it cool. "Deal."

"Aye," she said, leading him out of the room. "Now spill yer guts before I do."

Chapter Twenty-Six

A nita brought Joey to the storage room. It was a dark room, filled with barrels, crates, and other supplies. It was very disorganized with cobwebs on the wall. A cannon was near the front, pointing out toward the ocean. Joey was repulsed by the odor. It smelled like dead rats covered in urine.

Anita revealed the three pistols she had strapped across her chest to discourage any misbehavior. She unlocked his handcuffs and pushed him into the room. "Find the cannon balls and gunpowder, and hurry with it."

As his eyes adjusted to the darkness, he started looking in crates to find the supplies.

"Get to talking, how can I get me ship?" she demanded.

"Because you plan to live on the ship," Joey began, "I'm going to guess that financing a boat is like getting a mortgage on a house. The process is probably a little different, but this will give you the general concepts. There are special deals for first-time home buyers."

"I be likin' deals," she said.

"Most people do. As you know, if you want to buy a $200,000 house, you don't need the full $200,000. You would usually only need about $40,000 for the down payment."

"But I told you, I don't have the twenty percent to put down." She looked discouraged. "I need this bigger ship to get a good man. Do I need to fill up me treasure chest more?"

"Men certainly do like big and full treasure chests. But there are other options. You might be able to put down much less than twenty percent."

Anita leaned in closer.

Joey opened a crate. Inside he found bread and other rations. "As a warning, the drawback to putting less than twenty percent down is having to pay private mortgage insurance, abbreviated PMI. This could add over a half percent per year onto your payments, which is significant."

"But that be me only option," she objected.

"Then an FHA loan could work. It only requires three and a half percent down."

"Only three and a half percent?" she exclaimed. Some of the stress disappeared from her face.

"Yes, it is much less than twenty percent. It works well if you don't have great credit." He paused. "Do you know what a credit score is?"

Anita had no idea what a credit score was, but didn't want to appear ignorant. "Aye."

"Do you have a good score?"

"Of course I be having a good score!" she said reactively, offended that there should be anything bad about her. She again didn't want to admit to her ignorance.

"In that case, you might be able to qualify for a conventional mortgage through Fannie Mae. The rates can change over time, but you might be able to only put down three percent or five percent."

"Three percent would be great." A sinister look flashed across her face as she thought about being able to quickly get a new, more powerful ship. "Out of all these options, which one should I do?" she asked.

He opened another crate, which was full of ropes. He felt something on his foot. When he looked down he saw a rat running across his shoe. A shiver went through his spine and he moved toward the back of the room. "It really depends. Ask your banker which one is the best for your situation." He paused as he thought of another option. "Too bad you're not a military veteran. They can sometimes forego the down-payment altogether."

"Veterans?" She became excited. "Those be the men wearin' uniforms? Who protect others with their big guns and dedication to a higher cause?"

"Yes," he said, wondering where she was going with this.

She brushed her fingers through her hair. "I love men in uniform. They don't need to buy a place, they can live with me for free."

"I'm sure they would love that," Joey said sarcastically under his breath. "Some people think they just need cash for the down payment, but there are several other costs."

"Why's it matter?"

"Because many people I know didn't factor in these costs. They scrambled to get enough cash at the last minute, or they had to use high-interest credit cards. You'll need cash for the appraisal, earnest money, closing costs, moving costs, new furnishings, and the home inspection."

"Inspection? What a waste of treasure."

He shook his head. He was surprised how often he heard this comment. "No, it isn't. One couple I knew skipped the inspection so they could save a few hundred dollars. They thought the house looked fine. Then a few months later, they found a crack in the foundation and discovered it was full of termites. It was a very expensive mistake."

She gazed out the small circular window. "I'd happily live with termites if it meant having a man in me life."

Joey hoped that man wouldn't have a wooden leg. He smiled at the thought.

"How much cash will I need then?" she asked.

"Plan on having at least 7% of the purchase price in cash. If you are buying a place for $150,000, you would need about $10,000 of cash. This should cover both the down payment and all the other expenses you will need cash for."

She seemed to be doing a calculation in her head.

He examined the row of barrels next to a pile of wood. One of the barrels had "gun powder" printed on the side. "There are a lot of things to consider when buying a home, so make sure you do your research."

"What kind of research? I don't have time for that."

"Then make time. It will probably be the biggest purchase of your life, so read a few books on the topic. Google things like 'advice for first-time home buyers' or 'common mistakes when buying a home'. Ask for advice from people who recently went through the process."

"Why should I do all the work? Can't someone just teach me?"

"Actually, there are probably organizations in your community that give free in-person courses. The point is don't be ignorant when you start house shopping." He opened another crate and quickly shut it, repulsed by what was inside.

She sighed. "I guess you be right. How big of a ship can me buy? The bigger the better."

"An important lesson is to buy less home than you can afford. Realtors and bankers might tell you that you can afford a bigger home. But keep in mind, the more you spend, the more they make. Trust your own judgment. You can always upgrade in a few years."

"Trust me judgment? I don't know anything about budgeting. Give me an estimate; about how much can I spend each month?"

Joey looked behind some crates. He saw several dead rats, with flies flying around them. He had to run away from the smell. After breathing in some less-repugnant air, he continued. "In general, don't spend more than 35% of your after-tax income on housing-related expenses."

She waved her hand dismissively. "I don't be needing to do all that math. Since I know I can afford me monthly rent, I'll just have me mortgage payment equal that."

"No," he warned. "People assume that if they're paying $1,500 in rent that they can afford a $1,500 mortgage payment. That's a mistake. When you own your own place, you have extra expenses that you don't have when you rent."

"Like what?" she asked.

He turned the corner around a stack of crates and ran into a row of slaughtered pigs hanging from the ceiling. He snapped back and wiped an unknown liquid from his face. "As an owner you have to pay property tax, home owner's insurance, repairs, utilities, home owners' association fees, private mortgage insurance, and more. These extra costs can add over thirty percent onto your mortgage payment."

She thought over the numbers. "Thirty percent be a lot, but I should be able to afford those extra expenses. If not, then I'll just do more pillaging."

While Joey didn't respect the way she earned her extra income, he admired the fact that she could get more money whenever she pleased. "In that case, here is something to consider. Suze Orman recommends 'playing house' for six months before you buy a place. Figure out how much your mortgage, insurance, taxes, and other expenses will cost. Put the extra amount you will need into a savings account on the first of each month. Pretend it's a bill."

"Why would I want to do that?"

He opened another crate. To his relief, he found cannon balls inside. "To see how it goes. Is it easy to come up with the extra money each month, or are you struggling? It's better to find out before locking yourself into a thirty-year mortgage. And that savings account can then help with the down payment or other expenses." Joey dragged the barrel and crate to the front of the room.

"I don't be likin' those other expenses, and I don't like you lecturing me." Anita chained Joey next to the cannon. She rolled the cannon away from the wall, an evil smirk on her face. She pointed it directly at him. Joey's face turned to a look of horror as he stared down the barrel of the cannon.

CHAPTER TWENTY-SEVEN

Anita looked at Joey, the cannon pointed directly at him. "Load it," she commanded.

"Huh?" he asked in confusion.

"Load the cannon, you blowfish snorter."

Joey breathed a sigh of relief. "How do I do that?"

She cursed his ignorance, then loaded the cannon herself while he watched. "What else do I need to know about me mortgage?"

Joey shifted his mind back to finance. "Over time, more of your payment will go toward paying down the principle. However, it could take over ten years before the amount you pay in interest equals the amount you are paying toward principle."

"What do you mean?"

"On a $200,000 mortgage at 3.6% interest, the monthly payment is around $900. After your first payment, how much will you still owe the bank?"

She motioned for him to grab some powder and cannon balls. He carried the heavy load, grunting in pain as he did. His shoulder and leg weren't fully healed yet. They left the room. "$200,000 minus $900, which equals $199,100," she answered as if the answer was obvious.

"Nope," he said. "Your principle balance is only reduced by around $300."

"But the payment was $900," she objected.

"I know. The other $600 you paid goes to the bank as interest. This adds up. Over the life of the loan, you'd pay over $127,000 in interest on top of the $200,000 you borrowed."

"That be an outrage!" They left the storage room and entered a wooden hallway. "That's too much to pay in interest. How can I pay less?"

They entered another room. There were two black cannons inside. The first was old and dirty, the other shiny and new. "You can make half-payments every two weeks rather than one monthly payment. This will save you interest and you'll pay off the mortgage faster."

"How that be?"

He took some water and washed out the inside of the dirty cannon. "There are fifty-two weeks in a year. By making twenty-six half-payments, you end up making thirteen full payments. When making monthly payments, you only make twelve full payments. You can pay off your mortgage five to ten years early by doing this."

"I be liking that."

"Yes, just check with your bank first. Some charge extra fees for it, so be careful." He grabbed a nearby piece of cloth and dried the cannon. He loaded the powder, then carefully rolled the ball inside.

"Aye," she said. "So whenever I come across extra treasure, I should pay down the mortgage with it?"

"Not necessarily." He loaded the next cannon in the same way.

"Interest rates for mortgages are really low right now. You also get a tax benefit from the mortgage payment. Pay off your credit cards and build up a six-month emergency fund before paying extra on your mortgage."

"Ah." She seemed more comfortable with the idea of a mortgage. She led him up to the main deck.

"Another thing you should consider is what type of mortgage you want."

"There be different kinds?"

"Yes, there are two main types of mortgages: fixed rate and adjustable rate. Even though adjustable rate might be cheaper today, you should consider a fixed-rate mortgage."

"Why would I want to pay more?" She motioned to an ornate brass cannon.

Joey looked at the intricate designs on the cannon and admired the craftsmanship. "Interest rates are low and are expected to rise, so you want a fixed rate. While an adjustable rate mortgage is cheaper in the short-term, it could end up being much more expensive in the long run if interest rates increase." Joey grabbed some gunpowder. The smell of it caused him to sneeze, making it get all over his face. He tried to wipe it off.

"Anything else?"

Joey pondered her question as he finished loading the cannon. "There are obviously a lot more things we could talk about. But I think we covered the main points."

Ivan and Macon walked over. They scowled at Joey.

Joey stared back, unblinking. Although he wasn't usually a confrontational person, he found the encounter exhilarating.

Ivan addressed Captain Goodman. "We be here."

She smiled. "Perfect timing." She walked to the edge of the boat and gazed at the nearby land.

Joey followed her gaze and saw a peaceful town in the distance. He saw simple homes and cobblestone streets. A charming wooden bridge was built over a gentle flowing stream. The scene looked familiar to him but he couldn't remember why.

Anita looked lustfully at the town. "Ready the cannons."

"What!" asked Joey. "You can't fire on this town. What did they do to you?"

"This be the hometown of your Captain Rich R. Dailey."

Joey turned to look at the town again and instantly recognized it. He hadn't seen it in what seemed like decades, but memories quickly returned to him.

She stroked the cannon in front of her. "It be time to send the world a message that I'm the most powerful pirate on the high seas now. That will cause all the men to admire me, and be a blow against Rich."

Joey felt he had to figure out a way to save this town, but he wasn't sure why it was a target to begin with. "Why do you hate him so much?"

She scoffed. "Because he ruined me life. He made me lose me man and me job."

"Your job?" asked Joey surprised. "Are you the crewmate he fired?"

"Aye, it be me. When I be at me lowest point, losing the love of me life because of him, he kicked me when I be down and fired me." She gritted her teeth in anger. "I fell into a deep depression after that. But then I recovered and vowed to find an even better man, and make Rich pay for what he did."

"Aye," exclaimed Ivan. "She decided to take on the mighty Captain Dailey, and she be winning."

She nodded. "I may not be the smartest pirate, and I may not always know what I be doing. But I be workin' hard and take decisive action. That's what allows me to succeed. I already be havin' the fiercest reputation on the sea, which I built in a short amount of time. And that be just the beginning." She looked toward the town. "Now it be time to teach him a lesson." She smiled at Joey. "And you'll be firing the first shot."

Joey backed away, waving his hands. "I'm not doing that."

"As me prisoner, yes you will. You'll already have blood on your hands since you loaded the cannons that will cause this town's destruction."

Joey's face turned pale. Ivan pushed Joey toward the brass cannon, then lit a torch and shoved it into Joey's hand. Ivan pushed Joey's arm down to the fuse, but he resisted with all his might. He pushed his legs against Ivan, trying to get away from the cannon, but Ivan held firm.

Joey looked at the peaceful town. He needed to think quickly about how he could get out of this situation. "Wait a second," he said to Anita. "You're right, if you destroy this town, guys will respect you. But do you know what they like even more?"

Anita said nothing but waited for the answer.

"A powerful woman with a big ship. Guys love women with impressive ships. My successful friends always say that."

Her eyebrows raised. "You be having successful friends? Will you introduce me?"

Joey was taken aback by this request. "I guess so, but not if you make me destroy this innocent town."

She thought about his offer. "Fine, no destruction of the city."

Ivan stomped away in anger, cursing. Joey breathed a sigh of relief. His grip relaxed on the torch he held in his hand.

Anita walked toward the stairs. She then turned around, grabbed Joey's arm, and before he could react, forced his arm down to light the cannon. He tried to resist, but the deed was done. He stood in horror as the explosion rocketed the cannon ball toward the town.

Ivan and Macon cheered. They ran to fire the other cannons.

"How dare you trick me like that!" shouted Joey.

Anita sneered at him. "That's not all I be trickin' you on. You signed the death warrant on your father as well."

Joey stood there confused, but felt the anger rise inside him.

"You be thinking I want a bigger ship to attract men quickly. But, I actually be needing it for a different reason. I'm gonna use it to destroy Captain Dailey, once and for all. When he comes to rescue you tonight, my new, more powerful ship will be there, waiting in surprise. I didn't know I could afford the ship before. But you be solving that problem with your ever-so-detailed instructions." An evil laugh bellowed from deep within her.

Joey's blood began to boil. "You two-faced liar!"

"Don't you dare call me a liar, ye pox-faced scurvy swabbie. I told you a half-truth. I still think having a bigger ship will get me a better man. In fact, I'd probably take a good man over getting revenge on your father. But for now, I will take his destruction. And I'll take great satisfaction knowing you helped bring it about."

Joey lunged forward to attack, but Ivan and Macon restrained him.

"Take him back to his cell. I'm off to the bank to get me a ship with twice as many cannons as me current one." A venomous sneer crossed her face.

Joey struggled to get free from their grip, but was unsuccessful. Macon put the handcuffs on him, purposely catching skin between the metal when clamping them down. As they dragged him to the cell, Joey caught a glimpse of the town. Smoke was everywhere, and the once-charming bridge was now nothing but rubble.

Chapter Twenty-Eight

She be sailing like new," exclaimed Captain Dailey. The salty air blew through his beard as the ship sailed the ocean's waters. They had spent the past couple hours patching the damaged ship, finishing just as the sun was setting. Though it needed more work, the ship was in pretty good shape.

They sailed toward the small island.

Sandy grabbed a brass spyglass. She extended it to look at the island. After a minute of searching, she became worried. "Captain, I don't be seeing them."

The captain took the spyglass and looked through it. "Where they be?" He looked through it again. "Lower the rowboat," he ordered.

The captain and Sandy boarded the rowboat and soon arrived on the island.

"Ahoy? Joey! Owen!" shouted Sandy.

"Over here," replied Owen in a disheartened tone.

They jogged toward the voice. After searching high and low, they called again. "Owen?"

"Here," he said.

They found him tied to the tree. Sandy ran over to untie him.

"What happened? Where be Joey?" asked the captain.

Timidly, he said, "Captain Goodman took Joey as a hostage."

"No!" shouted Sandy, burying her head in her hands.

The captain clenched his fist. "How could you let this happen?" he demanded of Owen.

Owen lowered his head. "They set up this booby-trapped treasure chest and caught us in a net. We be unarmed when they came."

"What happened next?" he demanded.

"They were going to kill me, but Joey be a brave lad. He offered himself as collateral and saved me from certain death."

"Collateral for what?"

Owen became silent.

"Collateral for what?" the captain repeated.

"I took a loan from Captain Goodman."

The captain shook his head in disbelief.

"Owen, how could you?" asked Sandy.

"I'm surprised you still be alive," said the captain

"The only reason I be alive is to give you the message," Owen said.

The captain tensed up.

Owen continued, "You must deliver the map to her midnight, or she is going to kill Joey."

"No!" shouted Sandy.

The captain gritted his teeth. He thought about the map, the curse, and the evil Captain Goodman. Then he got an idea that made him smile. "I think it be time to teach her a lesson she won't soon be forgettin."

CHAPTER TWENTY-NINE

Joey paced his cell. His emotions shifted between anger for Anita and sorrow for the innocent town. As his anger bubbled up again, he tried to focus on other things, knowing that he needed a clear head to get out of this situation.

He decided to take advantage of his time being imprisoned to reflect on his life and career. He rarely had any free time for reflection anymore. With his busy schedule, there was always another project to work on, meeting to attend, email to check. He was doing well financially, but was he on the right track? Did he have the right priorities? Was there more to life than just a successful career and making money? Was he happy?

The crewman with the medallion came down. He tip-toed to the cell with a tray of food. "Here ya go, matey." He slid the food in between the bars. "I'm not supposed to be feedin' ya. But I feel bad about your predicament, and regret being mean to ya before. I figured you'd be hungry, so I brought you one of me favorite dishes."

Joey was starving. The plate was full of vegetables and a choice cut of meat. He ate the food quickly and drank the glass of water in one gulp. Not only was it delicious, but healthy too.

"Thanks," said Joey. "What's your name?"

"I be Eaton Wright."

"Well, I appreciate it. You are pretty fit; you must eat like this all the time."

"I be taking my health seriously. Exercising regularly keeps me feeling good and full of energy."

"Yes, that's very important." Joey remembered reading a *Forbes* article in which they asked twenty questions to a dozen self-made billionaires. Every single one of them said they exercised several times per week. He made a mental note to emphasize to the crew the positive correlation between exercise and success, assuming he survived the night.

Eaton looked toward the stairs after hearing a creak. "I better be going." He hurried out of the room.

Joey's thoughts were interrupted by shouts coming from above. Anita had returned.

He immediately became angry again. How dare she trick him like that? He heard her come stomping down the stairs. He looked forward to seeing her and vowed to give her a piece of his mind. He wouldn't allow her to treat him this way, and he planned to let her have it.

She entered the room, her face red with anger. She pointed her finger at Joey like a dagger.

He didn't wait for her to speak, adrenaline rushing through his veins. "Listen here, you wretched wench! I've never met such a..." He stopped talking as she reached for her pistol.

"You conniving trickster," she steamed. "Think you can make a fool of me, aye? No one makes a fool of Captain Goodman!"

Confusion showed on his face.

She drew her pistol and pointed it at his head.

"Wait! What are you talking about?"

"Too late, you be out of luck now."

She cocked the pistol.

His anger had quickly turned to fear. "Please, wait! At least tell me what I did."

"You be disrespectin' me! That's one thing I not be tolerating."

"What? How did I disrespect you?" He racked his brain trying to figure out what he could have done.

"Playing me for a fool by saying I could get approved for a mortgage, even when you knew I'd be rejected. When that handsome banker told me the bad news, I be mortified. I've never been so embarrassed. Now you're going to pay the price!"

"Wait, I didn't know you'd be rejected, I promise," he pleaded. "What did he say?"

"Don't be acting ignorant now. You knew they'd reject me because of me low credit score, and you let me go off anyhow."

"Wait you told me—"

"Don't try to blame this on me, ya scurvy rat!" She thrust her pistol forward in a menacing way.

"Wait, I'm not blaming you! But you told me you had a good credit score."

She scowled at him. "No, I didn't. I don't even know what a credit score be."

He threw up his hands. "But you did, remember? You yelled at me for implying you wouldn't have a good score."

She lowered her pistol. She squinted her eyes, trying to remember.

"Either way, I can help you improve your credit score."

She paced back and forth. "What's it matter now? I can't get me new ship before tonight anyway." She lowered her head, looking dejected. She continued pacing, then stopped. "But I know what would make me feel better." She looked at him hungrily. "Yes, torturing you until you be nothing but a pile of skin and bone on the floor." She walked to the chest in the corner of the room.

Joey's stomach dropped. "Wait a second. You don't want to do that."

She ignored his comment and opened the chest.

He figured he needed to emotionally connect to her deepest need in order to survive. He desperately tried to think of what to say. "You want a quality guy, right?"

She stopped and looked at him, saying nothing.

"Those guys love girls with big and powerful ships. You know it is true." He hoped with all his heart that she actually did think it was true, or he was a dead man.

She seemed to nod her head while she thought over his comment. "Aye." She rubbed her chin. "I be needing a bigger ship," she said as her voice trailed off.

"And I can help you get it," he said quickly. "I can tell you how to improve your credit score."

She walked away from the chest. "Get talking, boy, before I change me mind. It be a long day, and I need a nap before the battle."

He nodded and leaned forward. He figured it was safe for him to give her detailed instructions. It takes months to improve a credit score, not hours. By then he hoped this whole ordeal would be behind him. "When it comes to qualifying for a mortgage, there are three main factors they look at: the debt-to-income ratio, loan-to-value ratio, and credit score."

She gave him a confused look.

He continued. "Banks care about the debt-to-income ratio because they want a borrower to have a small amount of debt and a large amount of income. A borrower with those characteristics is more likely to pay back the loan. Therefore, you want a low debt-to-income ratio."

She still looked confused.

"Let's take an example. How much do you make each month before taxes?"

"5,000 doubloons."

"If you add up all the minimum payments you have to make each month, how much is that?"

She thought about her payments. "I pay four debts each month; they total 1,200 doubloons."

"To calculate the debt-to-income ratio, simply take 1,200 doubloons divided by 5,000 doubloons. This equals 0.24, so your debt-to-income ratio is 24%."

"Do that be good?"

"In general you want this number to be below 28%, so yours it good."

"Then why did he reject me?" She said under her breath, "Story of me life, men always rejecting me."

"Because banks look at more than just your debt-to-income ratio. Next is the loan-to-value ratio, abbreviated LTV. This shows how much the bank is lending against an asset. If they loan a lot of money against a house, that is riskier for the bank. They want to give you a small loan on an expensive house. That is because the house is acting as collateral for the mortgage. If you default and don't pay back the loan, they can foreclose on your house to get their money back."

"You be knowing firsthand about collateral, don't you?" she smirked.

Joey grimaced. He thought of Owen and hoped the captain had untied him from the tree by now. "Basically, you want your loan-to-value ratio to be low in order to get approved. Let's take another example. How much do you want to spend on your ship?"

"250,000 doubloons."

"How much would you need to borrow?"

"230,000 doubloons."

"230,000 is the loan amount, and 250,000 is the value of the asset. To calculate the loan-to-value ratio, take 230,000 divided by 250,000. This equals 0.92, so your LTV is 92%."

"Do that be a good number?"

"In general, you want this number to be below 80%. 92% is high. However, you're trying to do an FHA loan or conventional mortgage. Since those types of mortgages might only require 3% or 5% down, a high LTV should be okay."

"Enough babbling then! Get to the credit score already," she demanded. She walked over to the chest, opened it, and looked inside.

He looked in fear at the chest. "I've heard over seventy percent of people get rejected for a mortgage. The most common reason for the rejection is a low credit score, so rest assured you aren't alone. What's your score?"

"580."

Joey cringed at hearing this. "Oh yeah, that is really bad." He thought about it a little longer. "Downright horrible, actually."

"That isn't nice!" She didn't like how something she knew

almost nothing about was causing her to feel pain and guilt. She yanked out a red bag from the chest. "What's a good score then?"

"The credit score is also called the FICO score. It ranges from 300 to 850. The median credit score in America is around 725. You want yours to be over 760 to qualify for the lowest rates."

"I be wanting my score to be higher, higher than the crow's nest."

"Do you pay your bills in full and on time?"

"No," she said hesitantly.

"Start doing that. Any institutions you have credit with will report to the credit bureaus. These include colleges, credit card companies, car dealers, banks, cell phone companies, electric power companies, and so on. When they report that you didn't pay your bills on time, it hurts your credit score."

"Companies be tattling on me for not paying me bills?" She opened the bag and pulled out a black leather whip that had nine tails. Each tail had three hard knots tied to the end.

Joey wanted to say the companies had every right to report on her; after all, she received a service for which she didn't pay. But he decided to keep his mouth shut after seeing the whip. "Do you have low balances on your credit cards and loans? Or are you near maxed out on everything?" he asked hesitantly.

"Maxed out," she said, now feeling even worse about her financial situation.

"That also hurts your credit score."

"Apparently, I need lots of treasure to have a high score." She snapped the whip repeatedly; the tails cracked in the quiet room. She was gracefully devastating at handling the lashing instrument.

Joey gulped. "Luckily, that's not true. A good credit score is not about how much money you make. It's about how responsible you are with the money you have. There are people who make very little money with great credit scores, and there are millionaires with horrible credit scores."

She seemed more hopeful. "How can I raise mine?"

"Credit scores are a complicated topic. Don't try to fix your score without first doing significant research. Things you think would be good or bad could actually have the opposite effect."

"When the banker rejected me, I threatened to slash his stomach. Does that hurt me credit score?"

"Um, no. I don't think so."

"Aye, that be good." She returned the whip to the chest. "What be having opposite effects?"

"In some cases, paying off a credit card and cancelling it could hurt your score. Sometimes opening a new credit card and spending on it could actually help your score. People think going into overdraft on your checking account hurts your score, but that doesn't affect it at all."

"Those landlubbers be making things so confusing. How are you supposed to know what to do?"

"The best way to find out how to improve your credit score is go to the source. Just have FICO tell you."

"FICO? Do he be a good man? Do he have a liking for pirates?"

"FICO isn't a person, it's a company."

"Argh, that figures," she said. She pulled out a pear-shaped piece of metal with a screw at the top.

"FICO calculates your credit score. You actually have three different credit scores."

"Three?" she asked.

"Yes. That's because there are three credit reporting agencies: Equifax, Experian, and TransUnion. Each one calculates its own score for you."

"Which one did that scurvy banker use?"

"Banks will often use the middle score when deciding your mortgage rate."

"I better be finding out me scores. How can I find out the three of them?"

"You can buy your Equifax and TransUnion score on myfico.com. Go there and pay the $20 to find out your score. You cannot buy your Experian score; only banks can get that. All three scores should be similar, so if they aren't, you'll want to investigate why."

"Well, mine be low, and you still haven't told me how to improve it. Your time be up. Get ready to feel this inside you." She walked toward him, turning the screw. The pear-shaped object opened up like a rose, revealing four metal pieces that angrily and slowly spread apart from each other.

Chapter Thirty

Captain Dailey sat in his captain's quarters. On his desk sat a list of everything he knew about the curse. Next to it laid a list of everything he knew about Captain Goodman. He thought over his plan, playing through the different scenarios in his head. He felt his confidence growing.

"Captain!" shouted Sandy from above.

He got up from his chair. He snatched the map and hid it inside his coat pocket. He grabbed his cutlass and a sharpener and headed to the main deck. He walked over to Sandy. "What it be?"

"Look." She pointed to the burning town.

His heart sank. He grabbed the spyglass and examined the damage. Anger built inside him. He lowered the spyglass and reached for the sharpener. He paced back and forth, sharpening his blade. He was more determined than ever to bring Captain Goodman's reign of terror to an abrupt end.

"Wait!" Joey backed away from the pear-shaped torture device, his heart racing. "Just buy your credit score report from myfico.com! There's a section with specific suggestions on how to improve it."

Her eyebrows narrowed. "Do that be it?"

"Yes! Just follow their instructions," he stammered. She was still holding the object and pointing it at him. Sweat was dripping from his brow. "It takes the guess work out of trying to figure it out on your own." He held his breath, hoping his answer satisfied her.

She pondered his response. "Hmm." She scratched her chin. "That be simple enough." She lowered the device. He felt instant relief.

He figured the longer he talked, the longer he wouldn't be tortured. "Knowing your credit score is important," he continued. "But you also want to check your credit reports."

"They be different?"

"Yes, your credit score is a single number. But your credit report is several pages long. It shows your payment history and all your outstanding debt. You have a credit report with each of the three credit bureaus, and you should review each of them yearly."

"Why should I be wasting me time with that?"

"Because around 25% of credit reports have errors on them."

Her eyebrows raised in surprise. "How can there be errors on them if they be so important? Mine better not have any errors." She put the pear-shaped object back and rummaged around in the chest.

"The only way to know is to check."

"What kind of errors should I be lookin' for?"

"There are all kinds of errors that could happen. For example, you might pay all your bills on time but the reports say you don't. If you have a similar name as someone else, you might accidently have their information listed on your report. There might be a mislabeled bankruptcy. There could be liens listed that don't belong to you."

She shook her head. "I can't believe accidental mistakes could be on me credit report."

"Not all of them are accidental," warned Joey. "You also want to monitor for identify theft."

"I hate thieves, especially those who steal loved ones." She pulled out two wooden blocks connected by two screws. On each block was a row of metal spikes.

Joey turned his head away so he wouldn't have to look at the latest device. "Someone could have opened a credit card under your name and is spending on it without you even knowing."

This made her especially angry. "If someone be spending under me name, I'd keelhaul 'em."

He couldn't resist asking, "What is keelhaul?"

"It be where ye are tied to a rope, thrown overboard, and pulled underwater under the ship to the other side."

He rubbed his shoulder. "That doesn't sound pleasant."

"Yar, that's not all, matey. On the bottom of the ship be sharp barnacles. The victim is scraped against them, usually causing serious cuts or lost limbs."

Joey squinted upon hearing this. "Ouch!"

"Let it be a warning. No one better be taking out credit cards under me name."

"You better check, then."

"Aye." She tightened the screws. Her face lit up as the spikes came slowly together.

Joey's heart started racing. He tried to remain calm. "The good news is you can get your credit reports for free. You can access them once per year at annualcreditreport.com. This site was set up by the Federal Trade Commission and the three credit reporting agencies in response to the FACT Act. This federal law gives consumers free access to their credit report once per year. Use that official site. Don't go to those free credit report sites with all the commercials, since they often make you pay to sign up for a credit monitoring service."

She nodded and put the wooden blocks back in the chest.

"Do you know why having a high credit score is important?" asked Joey.

She answered instantly. "Because men think high credit scores be sexy?"

"No, I don't think any guy has ever said, 'Wow, check out the credit score on that girl.' But having a good credit score can save you a lot of money."

"Really?"

"Yes. Let's look at the 250,000 doubloon mortgage you want to take out for your ship. Say you take out a thirty-year fixed-rate mortgage."

"How much do that cost?"

"That depends on your credit score. Say you manage to increase your score to 620, which is better but still pretty bad. With that score, you could maybe qualify for a 6.2% interest rate. Your monthly payment would be about 1,500 doubloons. Over the course of thirty years, how much do you think you'd pay in interest?"

"Don't know, maybe 50,000 doubloons?"

"Is 50,000 doubloons a lot of money?"

"Yarr!"

"Well, you wouldn't pay 50,000 doubloons in interest. You'd pay 300,000 doubloons. That would be more than you paid for your ship."

"That be an outrage!" She pulled out a handsaw that was three feet long.

Joey's eyes widened at the length of the saw. He tried to keep his mind on the financial topic at hand. "Yes, it is a lot of treasure. If you manage to increase your credit score to 780, which is a great score, you might qualify for a 4.6% interest rate. With this lower rate you would pay less than 1,300 doubloons per month, which is 200 doubloons less than before."

"Having extra treasure to spend would be good."

"I agree. You'd also pay less in interest. Over the life of the thirty year loan, you would pay 210,000 doubloons in interest; this is almost 100,000 doubloons less than before. How would you feel with an extra 100,000 doubloons?"

"Happier than a powder monkey hornswoggling the hempen halter."

Joey noticed the pirates kept using that expression. He hoped he lived long enough to figure out what it meant. "Imagine if you invested that savings in the market over the thirty years. Your treasure chest would be overflowing."

"Aye, me matey. But thirty years be a long time to pay interest to the bank. I don't be liking that." She pulled out a file and filed the teeth of the saw, sharpening each tooth individually.

Sweat appeared on Joey's forehead. "The two main time frames are a fifteen-year and thirty-year mortgage. In general, I think the fifteen year is better if you can afford it. But you'll have to weigh the pros and cons to see what's better for you."

"Aye." She waited to see if he would say anything else. "So do that be all I need to know about credit scores?"

He worried that she would use that saw on him if he said yes.

He tried to think of something else to say to prolong his life. "Your credit score affects every area of your life. It affects the interest rates for your credit card, mortgage, and car loan. If affects your car insurance premiums. It affects if you can rent an apartment, if you will get hired for a job, and whether you can get a cell phone. Not only that, it can affect your love life."

"Love life?" she asked in surprise.

"Yes. My buddy wanted to marry his girlfriend. But when he asked her dad for his blessing, the dad said no."

"Why?" she asked, getting upset.

"Because my buddy had horrible money habits and a bad credit score."

Anita's jaw clenched. "How dare the dad get in the way of love like that." She filed the teeth even sharper.

"He just wanted what's best for his daughter, I guess," Joey said as he saw the blade glistening. "Just try to get your score above 760."

"But how's the score determined? Do someone just make it up?"

"Your FICO score is calculated with five factors." He thought about how to best show the information. "Think of it like a pie chart."

"I like pie." She put the saw back in the chest. "Tell me about the pie." She sat in the chair next to the cell.

Joey noticed the dirt on the wall. He drew a pie chart in the dirt with his finger.

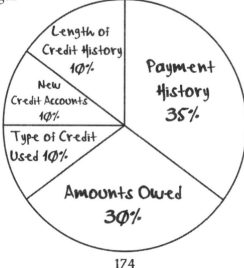

She wiggled in the chair to get more comfortable.

"This is how your credit score is calculated," he began. "The most important thing to do is pay your bills on time. This makes up thirty-five percent of your score. Being late just one time can significantly lower your score. It's a good idea to set up all your bills for automatic payment to make it easy on yourself."

"Aye, that be making sense," said Anita. She yawned.

"Thirty percent is made up of your credit utilization ratio. This is the amount you owe divided by your available credit. The theory is if you're maxed out on all your credit, you're more likely to file for bankruptcy. Keep this ratio below 50%. It's even better if you can keep it below 10% since that's what people with excellent credit scores do."

She began to blink slowly as if her eyelids were becoming heavier. "Aye."

"For example, if you have a credit card with a credit limit of $8,000, don't have a balance of more than $4,000. Ideally keep the balance below $800."

Joey noticed her eyes closing again. He then noticed her keys, which were within arm's length of his cell. He began to talk in a monotone voice. "The next item is the length of your credit history. This makes up fifteen percent of your score. It might make sense to open a credit card when you're a teenager to start building a credit history; just be sure to pay it off every time. Also, you never want to close your first credit card since that would reduce the length of your credit history."

Her head slowly lowered to her chest, then snapped back up.

"The next item is recent credit applications. This makes up ten percent of your score. The theory is that if you are applying for a lot of credit, that could mean you are in financial trouble. When someone asks to check your credit, ask them if it is a soft pull or a hard pull. A hard pull will slightly hurt your credit score for a few months, whereas a soft pull will not."

Her head lowered again, but this time didn't snap back up.

"The last and least important factor makes up ten percent. This is the mix of credit you have. Lenders like to see that you are able to handle many types of credit, such as a car loan, mortgage, bank credit card, retail credit card, college loan, and so on. But don't go into unneeded debt just to try to improve your credit score."

Judging by her breathing, Joey felt she was asleep. He saw the keys within grabbing distance. Should he reach for them? What if she awoke? What if he escaped but got caught? Was it safer to stay in the cell?

He weighed the risks and rewards of grabbing the keys. He finally decided to just go for it. Cautiously he reached for the keys. She moved in her sleep and he snapped back his hand. When she settled, he reached for them again. He was able to touch them. He carefully unhooked them from her belt while holding his breath.

He put the key in the lock and heard a click. He was scared and excited as he opened the door, careful to keep his eyes on her the whole time. She was sleeping comfortably.

He walked up the stairs when a thought crossed his mind that made him stop in his tracks.

CHAPTER THIRTY-ONE

Joey stepped forward, then snatched back his foot. He realized he didn't have a plan. He'd escaped from the cell, but now what? Even if he avoided being spotted by the crew, where was he supposed to go? He was in the middle of the ocean.

Realizing the futility of his efforts, he tiptoed back down the stairs. He had to get back into the cell and reattach the keys to Anita's belt before he got caught trying to escape. He walked to the cell and inserted the key. He then noticed the chest in the corner of the room. The thought of the toys she had inside made him shudder. He changed his mind again. He couldn't let her use any of those devices on him. He had to escape.

He tiptoed back to the stairs. He stepped on a wooden floorboard, and a creak was heard throughout the room. He froze. Anita shifted in her chair. His heart was racing, his face pale. She settled back into her chair and was again silent. He breathed a sigh of relief.

He got to the stairs, but what was he going to do now? He tried to remember what he saw when he boarded her ship. There were chests of equipment, cannons, a rowboat, sails, ropes, a door to the captain's quarters. Wait, a rowboat! He decided this was his best shot. He could keep rowing until a ship found him. He worried that he might die from dehydration before that happened, but he had to take the risk.

Slowly, Joey walked up the stairs. He peered over the top step. In the distance, he saw the rowboat sitting there unattended.

He looked around; he saw no one. This was his chance. He looked around one last time, then sprinted for the boat. He made it halfway to the boat without incident. His confidence rose.

"Hey, you there! Stop! Sound the alarms!" A loud bell rang furiously.

He darted forward even faster.

Anita ran up the stairs, looking around wildly. She spotted Joey sprinting toward the rowboat. "Get him!" she screamed.

Joey got in the boat and lowered the boat as fast as he could, but then felt four hands clamp down on him. Despite his struggling, he was pulled back onto the ship.

Ivan and Macon dragged him over to Anita.

"How dare you try to escape!" she fumed. She breathed heavily, a look of pure anger on her face.

She grabbed him by the arm, taking him to a wooden mast. "Time for ye to do the happy intestine dance."

Ivan and Macon cheered. Eaton and the other crewmate lowered their heads, as if trying to hide their eyes.

Joey didn't know what the happy intestine dance was, but he was sure it wasn't happy. He scrambled to think of a reason why she shouldn't hurt him. "Wait, I didn't finish telling you how to raise your credit score. Don't you want that new ship so you can get your dream man?"

"That won't be working this time, ye pox-faced scalawag," she spat.

"Do ye know what she's gonna do to ya?" asked Macon excitedly. "She's gonna copy Monbars the Exterminator's favorite form of torture." He smiled. "First, she's gonna cut open your stomach. Then she's gonna pull out one end of your intestines, which she'll nail to the mast. Then you're gonna dance around the pole happily until it all be unwound. And if ye don't dance, we'll beat ya with burning sticks until ye do."

Joey broke into a cold sweat. His heart raced.

Anita unsheathed her blade, eyeing his stomach. Ivan and Macon grabbed two wooden sticks from the supply chest and lit them on fire.

Joey's muscles tensed up as he froze in fear. His throat tightened and became dry. He couldn't move, staring at the fires burning in front of him.

"Get ready to dance, ye son of a biscuit eater." She pulled back her sword, ready to swipe at his stomach.

"Captain, captain!" shouted Eaton.

She looked at him angrily. "This better be urgent, or ye be next!"

"It's Captain Dailey. His ship be closing in fast."

Anita looked at Joey. She looked at her sword, gripping it tightly.

"Kill him before Captain Dailey gets here!" shouted Ivan.

She paused, her eyes staring like daggers into Joey. Then she turned away. "No, we can't be doing this yet," she said through clenched teeth. Reluctantly she said, "Get him out of me face. Take him back to the brig."

"Hoist the colors!" shouted Captain Dailey.

They raised his signature pirate flag into the night sky. It flapped briskly in the moonlight.

He saw Captain Goodman's ship ahead and became anxious to teach her a lesson she'd never forget. Her ruthlessness had gotten out of hand recently, but kidnapping his son was a new low. She had to be stopped, and only he could do it.

They were closing in quickly. Suddenly they saw flashes of light and heard blasts echoing around them.

"Cannon fire!" shouted Owen as they ran for cover. The side of their ship took the brunt of the damage.

"Return fire!" the captain shouted to Sandy.

She ran to the cannons, executing her duties as head gunner with precision. The projectiles rocketed toward Anita's ship with a fury that caused far more damage than their own ship had sustained.

"Steer the ship closer!" The captain knew he didn't have much time before the next round of blasts fired at him. As the ships converged, he shouted, "Prepare to board. Get the ropes!"

179

Owen steered the ships closer together. When the ships got next to each other, the captain commanded, "Board!" They grabbed their ropes and swung over to the unknown of the enemy ship.

Chapter Thirty-Two

Captain Dailey's crew swung across the chasm and boarded Captain Goodman's ship. They were tense and ready for battle.

Anita smiled in a sinister way. She walked over calmly. "If it isn't the great Captain Rich R. Dailey. It's been a while, hasn't it? Welcome to me ship."

"Where be me son?" he demanded.

"Oh, he be safe." A malevolent look flashed across her face.

"Where he be?" the captain demanded again.

"Where be Duarte's map?" she countered.

"First me son." He said it with a sternness that made it clear this was non-negotiable.

She looked at Eaton. "Alright you worthless slog, go get him."

Eaton went downstairs. A minute later he emerged with the prisoner.

"Joey!" shouted Sandy with puppy-dog eyes. She ran toward him but Owen held her back.

Anita gave Sandy a venomous look. She turned her attention to the captain and said, "Here be your boy." She unsheathed her sword and held it up to Joey, "and here be me cutlass. How ironic if I took your son from you like you took my fiancé from me?"

"I didn't take away your fiancé, Anita. And you know it," said the captain.

"Me name be Captain Goodman to you. And yes you did! You forced me on your treasure hunt, making me miss our anniversary dinner. If I hadn't been on your wild-goose chase, on a ship in the middle of nowhere, me fiancé never would have met the wench at the restaurant when I didn't show up! You made me lose the man of me dreams, and now I'll be alone forever!"

The captain shook his head. He tried to speak calmly. "You know I didn't be forcing you to go. I said you could go to your dinner."

Her face turned red with anger. "It's not what you said, it be how you said it. You be making it perfectly clear how you felt about me picking romance over work. And then after my fiancé left me for that biscuit-eating wench, you kicked me when I be down. You fired me from the crew, making me jobless and heartbroken." She raised her sword to Joey's throat.

"Leave him be, or I'll burn the map!" Captain Dailey shouted. "I already be apologizing a hundred times for you losing your fiancé. And I gave you a dozen warnings before I be firing you. You were reckless and destroyed the camaraderie of the crew. You sabotaged all the treasure hunts we did thereafter. You be leaving me no choice."

"Now you be having a choice." She gripped Joey's arm tightly, shaking him. "Give me the map or it'll be X marks the spot across his stomach."

The captain took a deep breath. "I be having a different idea. I challenge thee to a duel. Winner gets the map..." he paused, "and the other's ship."

Her eyes widened and pupils dilated. "Defeating the great Captain Dailey and taking your ship?" She looked at his ship lustfully. "I be lovin' nothing more. I accept."

They walked toward each other, and their crews surrounded them in a circle. Tensions rose as both captains unsheathed their swords.

Captain Dailey knew this was his opportunity to end the terror of Captain Goodman. For too long he had let her sail the seas unchallenged.

Anita knew that if Captain Dailey were taken down by her hands, her power would increase immeasurably. All the other pirates would realize that she was in control. She would be queen of the pirates, and it would then be easy to find her king. Thinking of the map, his ship, a real boyfriend and her uninhibited rule, she salivated.

Anita rushed forward and their blades clashed.

Sandy gasped at the clang of steel hitting steel.

Anita swiped her cutlass at the captain's head. He raised his sword to block the blow, which sent him stumbling backward.

Captain Dailey regained his stance and lunged forward, aiming at her stomach. She was nimble and spun to the right, hitting him in the back with the hilt of her sword. He turned and moved forward, swiping again. Their blades clashed and clashed again. Captain Dailey delivered a blow so forcefully that it caused Anita to lose her balance, making her to fall to the ground.

Owen, Rusty, and Sandy cheered for their captain, but he was too focused on the task at hand to notice. As Anita lay on the ground, he raised his cutlass to deliver the final blow. As the metal came crashing down upon her frightened body, she rolled away just in time, and his sword plunged into the wooden floor. He pulled on the blade to remove it from its entrenchment, but it was stuck.

Anita got up and saw her opportunity. As he wrestled to release his sword, she came from behind and swiped at the captain. He saw her hurtling toward him out of the corner of his eye. He jumped away, but it was too late. Her blade slashed into his arm, and the first blood was drawn.

Sandy screamed, "No!" The captain was forced to run. Anita saw him leave his protection behind and chased after him. Owen and Rusty ran to the embedded sword and heaved it out of the floor's clutches, then threw the cutlass to the captain. He caught the blade in time to block another attack from Anita.

The captain's wound was throbbing, but he fought through the pain. After several more blows they backed away, pacing back and forth while staring menacingly at each other. They tried to catch their breath.

"You be a weak old man," said Anita. "Admit defeat and save yourself the misery."

The captain was not influenced by her empty words. He caught

183

his breath, looked at his son who was tied up against the mast, and sprinted at her. This caught her by surprise. Even though she raised her sword to defend herself, the sheer momentum of his blow sent her reeling backward, making her drop her sword. The captain stomped his foot on her cutlass, preventing her from retrieving it. He prowled toward her, sword in hand, and she scrambled backward. With her running out of space to retreat any further, the captain had her cornered. He pointed his cutlass directly at her throat as she lay in front of him, defenseless. "You've lost, Anita. Admit defeat."

She pressed up against the side of the ship, trying to avoid his blade. She sneered. "I may have lost the battle, but it doesn't matter." She drew her pistol and pointed it at Joey. "Lower your blade or he dies."

The captain was shocked. "You can't be doing that. It be against the Code."

"I spit on the Code." She spat on the ground to emphasize her point. "Drop your blade!" She cocked her pistol.

He looked at his son and reluctantly dropped his sword.

She stood up. "You know, I be thinking this over. Killing your son with you standing here would greatly enhance me reputation for ruthlessness. Then after I kill him, I'll kill you too, and take the map from your cold, dead body." She felt warm inside at the thought of this plan. She turned to Joey. "Get ready to die."

"No!" yelled Sandy, tears streaming from her eyes. "Don't hurt him!"

Anita felt a sickly happiness knowing she would bring heartbreak to a beautiful young girl. She smiled. "Good-bye, Joey."

The captain yelled, "Wait! Here be your map." He waved it in the air. "Go get it!" He threw the map in the air and the wind carried it toward the side of the ship.

In panic, Anita ran to the map. It continued to flow in the air over the side. She thrust out her hand and snatched the map, just before it fell into the ocean's waters.

She stood there looking at it, eyes wide with greed. "I have it now. The path to the greatest treasure ever known be in me hands."

She began to breathe heavily and looked around at those lesser beings in her presence. She looked at Owen and noticed the way he was looking at the map. "Owen, I know you be wanting this as much as me. Join me. We can rule the seven seas together, each of us with more treasure than we can imagine. And both of us," she paused for emphasis, "as captain."

Owen took a deep breath upon hearing the word 'captain'. He looked at the map with a longing gaze. Finally he said, "A few days ago, I probably would've accepted ye offer. But after seeing the integrity and loyalty of the captain and Joey, I be realizing there's more to life than treasure. For what will it profit me if I gain the whole world but forfeit my soul?"

She sneered at him. "Whatever, be a fool then. It be time to see where this treasure be." Anita started to open the map, but hesitated.

"I wouldn't open that if I be you," warned the captain. He held his breath, as his plan depended on her taking the bait.

She looked at the map, then back at the captain. After a slight hesitation, she said, "Well then, it be a good thing you're not me." She tore open the map, eyes wide with excitement. She voraciously looked it over. Her excitement quickly turned to confusion, followed by anger. "What's this? What be the island of budgeting, and the straits of credit..."

They heard a loud, deep male voice echoing from the sky. "Scoundrel! You have opened the map without breaking the curse. You will now be punished for eternity, a captive of the sea."

Anita looked around, confused. "What? Who be saying that?"

To her shock, two skeletons crawled over the side onto the ship. They stood before her, dressed as pirates, but their clothes were torn and disheveled.

The captain had a satisfied look of surprise on his face.

Owen turned to the captain. "Maybe she can count as our willing sacrifice," he whispered hopefully. The captain said nothing but watched intently.

The two skeletons walked up to her. They took the map from her hands, folded it back up, and placed it gently in the supply chest.

They then returned to her, grabbed her forcefully, and dragged her toward the plank.

"Wait, what be this?" she shouted. "Where are you taking me? Stop! I'm not going anywhere." She dug her feet into the ship's deck. She flailed her arms, trying to escape their death grip.

"So much for the willing part," muttered Owen.

"Stop! Where you be taking me?" she demanded.

The taller skeleton said, "Your punishment be to rule over the undead sailors of the sea, for eternity. You be the sea's captive. Never again will ye set foot on dry land."

It took her a moment to process what he had said. "I'm gonna rule over all the sailors taken by the sea?" she asked.

"Aye."

"How many of them are there?"

"Thousands," the skeleton responded.

"Do these sailors still be wearing their uniforms?"

Captain Dailey tried to suppress the smile that had sprouted.

The skeleton took a moment to respond. "Aye."

Anita pondered this. "Since I be their ruler, I can make them do whatever me want?"

"Aye."

She took a deep breath, a smile forming on her face. "Can I make them give me massages and long, soft kisses?"

The two skeletons looked at each other and shrugged. "Ah, I guess so."

She became elated at the news. "At long last, I can again have a boyfriend in uniform, as many as me want." She hadn't been this happy in years. She looked at the skeletons and commanded, "Let's go, mateys, I be ready. Let's get this party started."

She jumped off the plank into the ocean, followed by the skeletons.

CHAPTER THIRTY-THREE

Ivan and Macon looked at the spot where Anita and the skeletons had stood just moments before. They looked at the captain's crew, seeing they were outmatched.

Owen stepped forward and drew his cutlass, pointing it directly at Ivan. Ivan and Macon looked at each other and turned to run. They ran to the rowboat, shoved it into the water, and jumped over the side of the ship.

Owen laughed. "I always knew those two be cowards without Captain Goodman around to protect them."

Sandy rushed over to Joey and untied him. "Joey, I was so scared for you." She brushed her hand through his hair. "I realized my life wouldn't be the same without you. You be okay?"

He looked into Sandy's eyes and felt her soft touch. "I feel great, better than I've ever felt before." He took a deep breath. "And you're the best buxom wench for me, Sandy."

She blushed. "Aw, thanks, Joey."

He shook his head. "My name isn't Joey."

"It's not?" She was worried he had a concussion, or that he had lost his memory due to stress.

"No. From now on, call me Giuseppe." He turned to the captain. "Joey is no name for a pirate. Right, Captain?"

The captain felt a rush of hope flow through him. "You be saying what I think you be saying?"

"Aye, aye." Giuseppe put his arm around Sandy in a warm embrace. He looked into the night sky, the stars twinkling above in the heavens. He felt the midnight breeze across his face, smelling the scent of the ocean's waters. The rush of adrenaline still coursed through his veins. "I haven't felt this alive in a long time." He looked at the captain with a twinkle in his eye. "Permission to join the crew, Dad?"

The captain had waited to hear those words all his life. He smiled. "Permission granted, son."

They walked to each other and embraced in a warm hug.

The captain looked around. "We be having another ship!" He looked at Eaton and his crewmate. "We be needin' additional crew members, if ye want to join."

They both stood at attention. "Aye aye, Captain," said Eaton. "I be in awe of ya ever since I first heard about ya. It'd be an honor to serve with ya."

"Same here, Captain," said the other crewman.

"Perfect." The captain turned to his son. "Someone be needing to command them and the ship. How does Captain Giuseppe sound?"

Having the title of captain excited Giuseppe. He pictured himself sailing the open seas, commanding his crew as they journeyed to new adventures. "I think it has a nice ring to it." He paused. "But I don't think I'm qualified to be a captain yet." He looked at Owen. "Honestly, I think Captain Owen Moore sounds better."

"Really?" said Owen in excitement. "I could finally be a captain?" He turned to Captain Dailey. "Do that be alright with you?"

"Aye aye, Captain Moore."

Owen smiled ear to ear. "Thank you, sir. This be a dream come true!" Owen couldn't remember being this happy in years.

Everyone smiled and happiness floated in the air around them.

Giuseppe walked over to the captain. "Congratulations on defeating Captain Goodman. The world will be better off without her."

"Aye. I'm glad it worked out," the captain said with a shrewd grin.

Giuseppe cocked his head. "Wait a second. Did you expect it to play out like that?"

The captain smiled. "I didn't know it'd be turning out exactly like that. But it was one of the scenarios I be hoping for."

Giuseppe looked at his dad with renewed respect. "Impressive. Nice work." Giuseppe patted him on the back. His dad embraced his son, a big smile on his face.

After additional congratulations were exchanged, Rusty said, "Too bad we couldn't figure out how to break the curse."

Owen looked at the plank. "Looks like we got our willing sacrifice, thanks to Captain Goodman."

"But we were also supposed to share the map's pieces of eight with our fellow crew," said Giuseppe.

"Didn't Captain Goodman say something about budgeting and credit after she looked at the map?" asked Sandy.

They stood in silence as they pondered this thought.

"Giuseppe, weren't you teaching the crew eight personal finance concepts? What if the pieces of eight be those, rather than gold?" asked the captain.

That thought hadn't occurred to Giuseppe before, but it made sense. According to the mermaid, Duarte had been a great teacher, and that was something he would have valued. "If that's the case, I've already shared those concepts."

They all looked at each other, thinking the same thing. "The curse might be broken," said Owen.

The captain went and grabbed the map. "I guess there be only one way to find out." He took a deep breath, and opened it.

"Wait!" shouted Giuseppe, but it was too late. The captain had already unfolded it.

They stood in fear, looking around. They looked at each other. They looked at the sides of the ship. They looked at the captain.

The minute of silence felt like hours. Captain Dailey shrugged. "I guess we broke the curse."

The crew cheered and celebrated. Rusty jumped up and down. Eaton clapped his hands. Owen put his arm around the captain, patting him on the back. The captain let out a sigh of relief that had been building for two decades.

Giuseppe walked over to Sandy, both of them smiling. The noise drowned out from around them as they became focused on just each other. Giuseppe put his hands on her hips and pulled her toward him. He brushed his hand through her hair, and they kissed for the first time.

The celebration continued for a while longer. After it died down, Owen asked, "What's the map say?"

Rusty asked, "Yeah, where be the buried treasure?"

The captain studied the map. He squinted as he tried to understand it. "It don't seem to lead to any buried treasure."

"Huh?" asked Owen, disappointed.

"How can that be?" asked Sandy.

The captain looked over the map again. "There be a note here from Duarte."

"What's it say?" asked Giuseppe. The captain read the note aloud:

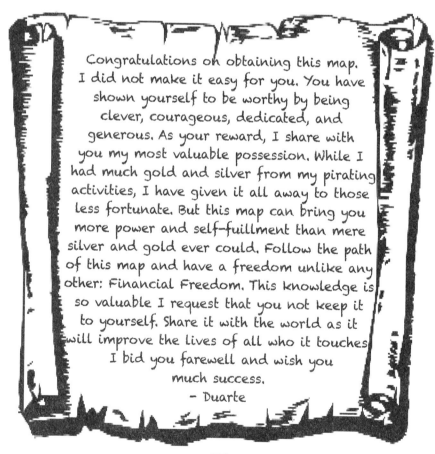

Congratulations on obtaining this map. I did not make it easy for you. You have shown yourself to be worthy by being clever, courageous, dedicated, and generous. As your reward, I share with you my most valuable possession. While I had much gold and silver from my pirating activities, I have given it all away to those less fortunate. But this map can bring you more power and self-fuillment than mere silver and gold ever could. Follow the path of this map and have a freedom unlike any other: Financial Freedom. This knowledge is so valuable I request that you not keep it to yourself. Share it with the world as it will improve the lives of all who it touches. I bid you farewell and wish you much success.
    - Duarte

"So there be no gold to find?" asked Owen.

"It appears not," said the captain. "Financial knowledge be the treasure. And he wants us to share it with the world."

The crew stood in silence, not sure what to think. Then Rusty said, "If that's what he be wantin', then that's what we'll be doin'."

The rest of the crew nodded in agreement.

The captain looked at the map. For years he had searched for it. Although the map wouldn't immediately bring him vast fortunes as he had hoped, he still felt a sense of accomplishment in having found it. He was happy that his hard work and persistence had paid off despite countless doubts.

"Duarte's right, you know," said Giuseppe. "If you found a treasure chest of gold, you would probably waste it away. Once it was gone, it would be gone forever. But when you have financial knowledge, you can make your own fortune and earn as much gold as you want. It truly is the ultimate treasure."

Rusty shrugged. "I guess," he said. "Duarte sure be different than the other greedy, no good, rotten pirates throughout history."

Giuseppe agreed. "You know what they say. Ninety-nine percent of pirates give the rest a bad name."

The crew laughed. Giuseppe chuckled as well, relieved that they had finally laughed at one of his jokes.

Rusty turned to Giuseppe. "You gonna teach us how to navigate this map now?"

"I would be happy to do that," said Giuseppe.

The captain looked at his crew, his map, and his son. He felt that all was right with the world. "Crew, it be time to celebrate. Get the rum!"

CHAPTER THIRTY-FOUR

A few years later...

Owen and Rusty were hanging out on the beach chatting. They saw Giuseppe and Sandy walking toward them, holding hands and looking very happy together. Giuseppe now had a well-trimmed chinstrap beard and goatee.

As they came closer, Rusty said, "Hey there, you love parrots."

"Hey guys," replied Giuseppe. "I haven't seen you both in months. How are things going on the other ship?" asked Giuseppe.

"Things be great, never been better," said Rusty.

Giuseppe saw Rusty had a parrot on his shoulder. "Is that Petey?"

"Yarr. And I could actually afford it based on your Ten Times Test."

Giuseppe smiled. "Nice work, Rusty."

"Thanks." It felt good to get a compliment from the same finance guy who'd been so hard on him before.

Rusty saw Sandy was wearing the opal necklace she'd wanted in the shop. "I see you be loosening up your wallet and buying Sandy some nice jewelry."

"I have certainly loosened up my wallet a bit," said Giuseppe. "It turns out there's more to life than budgets and financial responsibility."

"No kidding?" Rusty said with a smile.

"Yup, that's a lesson I learned from you, so thank you."

Rusty blushed.

"I realized it was a mistake to never spend money on fun things. Those things can bring you a lot of enjoyment. It's okay to buy things you don't need every now and then," continued Giuseppe. "You only get to be young once after all."

"Are you saying you're irresponsible with your treasure now?" asked Rusty in surprise.

"No, never. I'm still a stickler for being financially responsible. But rather than being that way 100% of the time, it's now closer to 90%."

"That be good to hear," said Rusty.

"Regarding the necklace, Sandy actually saved up for that all by herself. And I am really proud of her for it." He smiled at her and gave her a kiss. "But don't worry, I spoiled her by paying for her dream trip to the sandy shores of Huahine in French Polynesia. We had a great time."

"Oh yes we did," said Sandy as she slapped him on the rear. She gave him a kiss, biting him on the lip.

"Okay, settle down you two," said Owen with a smile. "Giuseppe, I know I be saying it before, but thanks again for ye help. Showing me how to read the map really got my finances in order."

"My pleasure, happy to help." Giuseppe looked at both of them. "So guys, anything new your way?"

Owen and Rusty smiled at each other.

"Aye. We have something to show ya."

"Okay, lead the way."

Owen and Rusty started walking; Giuseppe and Sandy followed.

"What do you have to show us?" asked Giuseppe.

"You'll see," said Owen.

They walked toward a well-hidden cave. Giuseppe wouldn't have noticed it if they hadn't pointed it out. Once inside, they lit some torches. The cave was empty.

Giuseppe looked around. "Yeah, this is a pretty cool cave, I guess."

Owen looked at Giuseppe with a puzzled look. "No, we haven't shown you anything yet." He walked to the side of the cave and rolled back a stone. Behind it was a secret room.

"Close your eyes," said Rusty.

Sandy and Giuseppe closed their eyes and were led inside.

"Ok," said Owen excitedly. "Open them."

They opened their eyes and were shocked at what they saw. There before them were three treasure chests overflowing with gold.

"Wow!" exclaimed Sandy.

Giuseppe couldn't believe his eyes. "This is amazing!" He looked at Owen and Rusty. "Did you find Blackbeard's treasure?"

"Blackbeard's treasure. Ha." Owen scoffed at the thought. "We be making our own treasure."

"Yep," said Rusty. "This be all ours, due to our own blood, sweat, and tears."

"Simply incredible," said Giuseppe.

"Best part is, I can be buying as much rum as me want now." Rusty walked over to his stash of rum in the cave, grabbed his favorite bottle, and poured a glass for everyone.

"The best part for me," said Owen, "is not feeling the weight of debt and uncertainty on me shoulders no more. I don't be owin' anything to anyone."

"Great job, guys. How did you do it?" Sandy asked excitedly.

"We be following the map, just like ya told us." Rusty had a big smile on his face.

"I am really proud of you both. Congratulations," said Giuseppe.

Captain Dailey entered the cave. "Aye, I be proud of ye too."

Owen and Rusty said together, "Thanks, Captain."

"And word be getting out," the captain continued. "We got landlubbers lined up and down the beach, wanting to join our crew." He looked approvingly at Rusty and Owen. "I think it be time for a third ship."

"That's exciting," said Giuseppe. "It sounds like things are going well for everyone."

"Aye, and me treasure be growing even faster than before. That map be having some good advice in it. Thanks again for all yer help, Giuseppe," said the captain.

"Anything for family," said Giuseppe.

Sandy looked at Giuseppe and smiled.

"Be it a hard process?" asked Sandy.

"It be hard at times. I ain't gonna lie, I be tempted to quit many times and go back to me old ways. But I stuck through it, rewarding meself along the way. And look what we've done."

They all admired the gold shining in the room.

"If a couple of simple pirates can do it, anybody can do it," said Rusty.

"Absolutely!" said Giuseppe. He raised his glass. "Everyone, here's to us being swash-buckling, rum-drinking, financially-free PIRATES!"

Together they exclaimed, "Argh!"

Bonus:
Goal-setting Guide

Congratulations on finishing this book! You have taken an important step in building the financial life of your dreams.

I hope you learned a lot about personal finance. But, I didn't write this book so you could learn about financial freedom. I wrote this book so you could actually achieve financial freedom.

The only way to do that is to take action. Far too many people already know the concepts in this book and have done nothing about it. Don't be one of those people.

If I did my job, this book should have inspired you to want to be financially free. You feel confident that you can achieve it. You see a path to make it happen. You are motivated to do whatever it takes to get there, not letting anything stand in your way. That is fantastic.

But I have bad news. Those feelings won't last. Other things in your life will come up to distract you from these desires. Your commitment will probably fade over time.

That is why we need to harness the power of your emotions today while you are still feeling inspired and unstoppable. The best way to do that, in my opinion, is to set goals.

What is the best way to set and achieve goals? I'm so glad you asked. I have spent significant time studying goal setting and have used many concepts myself. Entire books could be written on the topic, so I don't intend to cover all the aspects and nuances of the art of setting goals. But I will present you with what I feel is an effective way to accomplish what you want.

The first step is to figure out what you want. Have you ever thought about what your financial goals are? What does financial freedom look like for you? Now is the time to figure it out.

Next you should set a SMART goal. SMART is an acronym that has been around for many years. Goals should be Specific, Measurable, Ambitious, Realistic, and Time-bound. For example, "feeling less stressed about money," is not a SMART goal. However, "paying off $3,000 of credit card debt before my next birthday," is a SMART goal. Limit the number of goals you set since having too many will become overwhelming.

Great, so you have a goal. What are your chances of success? A lot of research has been done on goal setting. Not surprisingly, many people set goals around New Years. According to the University of Scranton's Journal of Clinical Psychology, only eight percent of people achieve their New Year Resolutions, and twenty-five percent give up on their goal within the first week. How can you improve your odds of success?

Write down your goal. Dr. Gail Matthews of Dominican University of California showed that people who wrote down their goals were about forty percent more likely to accomplish them.

Share your goals with others. According to the New York Times, sharing your resolution with another person makes you thirty percent more likely to achieve your goal. Forbes.com recommends posting your goals on the social media websites you use. This not only provides peer-pressure for following through on your goals, but when others read about your goals, they can cheer you on, offer their help, or even join you on your mission. Let them know what triggered this change in your behavior so it doesn't seem like it is coming out of nowhere.

Keep others updated on your progress. According to the Matthews study, participants who sent progress reports to their friends were 76.7% more likely to accomplish their goals.

Get an accountability partner. Or you can have several accountability partners and form a Master Mind group which was described by Napoleon Hill in his classic book *Think and Grow Rich*. Several studies have shown that people are twice as likely to achieve their goals if they have someone else involved in their journey. They can encourage you, help you brainstorm, correct you when you've gotten off track, provide accountability, and make it more fun. Just be sure to pick the right person; picking the wrong person can be more of a hindrance than a help.

Break up your goal into smaller pieces. The thought of accomplishing a big goal can be overwhelming. Instead, break it into many small parts that are easy to accomplish.

Evaluate your progress and revise direction if necessary. As you pursue your goals, surprises will come up, and things won't go as planned. That is okay. Be adaptable, and feel free to get help from others if you're not sure what to do next.

Fight through failures and don't give up. Obstacles and disappointments are part of the journey to success; every successful person has had failures at some point along the way. If you want to succeed quickly, fail faster. You and you alone are in control your success or failure. The only way you can truly fail is to quit.

Staying motivated through tough times can be challenging. Listening to upbeat music has been a huge help for me. Bouncing to the music while on my computer, even occasionally getting up to dance around, has allowed me to work for hours at a time and have fun while doing it. Listening to Tony Robbins has also helped me stay motivated.

Okay, so you have the principles for setting and achieving goals. Let's put it all together into an easy-to-follow process.

Step One: Set one or two SMART goals which take between a few months and a year to accomplish. Set them right now. If you need more time to think of a worthy goal, then set the goal of coming up with your goals within two days.

Step Two: Write down your goal and post it as a status update on your social media sites. If you understandably don't want to disclose sensitive financial information on those sites, you can make the posts vaguer than your actual goals.

Examples include:

- I just finished a personal finance novel. Now I'm committed to having $1000 in my emergency fund within three months. Feel free to encourage me along the way!
- If the Pirates of Financial Freedom can do it, so can I. I intend to be debt-free by the end of the year! If you're serious about it too, join my accountability group.
- Today is the start of my new financial destiny! In honor of the pieces of eight, I'm setting the goal of making $8,888 of extra income by Labor Day. Have any advice on how I can do it?

Step Three: Get an accountability partner or form a Master Mind group. Set a specific day, such as Sunday, and meet with them weekly. Each week set bite-sized SMART goals that will lead you to your big goal. Then the following week, discuss if you accomplished your goals, and set goals for the next week.

That's it. Do this now. Right now. And enjoy a life of financial success.

Reader's Notes

READER'S NOTES

READER'S NOTES

Reader's Notes